THE EXPERIMENTS

*The Bayou Hauntings
Book Five*

Bill Thompson

Published by
Ascendente Books
Dallas, Texas

This is a work of fiction. The events and characters described herein are imaginary and any reference to specific places or living persons is incidental. The opinions expressed in this manuscript are solely the opinions of the author. The author has represented and warranted full ownership and/or legal rights to publish all the materials in this book.
The Experiments: The Bayou Hauntings 5
All Rights Reserved
Copyright © 2019
V.1.0
This book may not be reproduced, transmitted or stored in whole or in part by any means, including graphic, electronic or mechanical without the express written consent of the author except in the case of brief quotations embodied in critical articles and reviews.
Published by Ascendente Books
ISBN 978-09992503-4-1
Printed in the United States of America

Books by Bill Thompson

<u>The Bayou Hauntings</u>
CALLIE
FORGOTTEN MEN
THE NURSERY
BILLY WHISTLER
THE EXPERIMENTS

<u>Brian Sadler Archaeological Mystery Series</u>
THE BETHLEHEM SCROLL
ANCIENT: A SEARCH FOR THE LOST CITY OF THE MAYAS
THE STRANGEST THING
THE BONES IN THE PIT
ORDER OF SUCCESSION
THE BLACK CROSS
TEMPLE

<u>Apocalyptic Fiction</u>
THE OUTCASTS

<u>The Crypt Trilogy</u>
THE RELIC OF THE KING
THE CRYPT OF THE ANCIENTS
GHOST TRAIN

<u>Middle Grade Fiction</u>
THE LEGEND OF GUNNERS COVE

This is my fifth book set in southern Louisiana, and the trips I take to Acadiana for research just get better and better. My friend David Crocker accompanied me on the journey this time, and we went from New Orleans up the River Road, across through Lafayette and down into Iberia Parish. I was on a search for ideas, a place for a ghost story to unfold, and a small town with a lot of history.

It was a cold rainy day when we drove across a drawbridge that spanned the Teche and entered the charming community of Jeanerette. Here was the town I'd been looking for! When we saw a grand antebellum home called Bayside Plantation on Old Jeanerette Road, its haunting beauty became my inspiration for the fictional Amelia House in this book.

I dedicate this one to the warm, friendly people of Iberia Parish. Laissez le bon temps rouler!

CHAPTER ONE

Amelia House Plantation
Jeanerette, Iberia Parish, Louisiana

Amelia House sat at the end of a narrow tree-lined lane off Old Jeanerette Road. As was the custom when building mansions in the days before automobiles, the front side of the house faced the river — Bayou Teche in this case. The owner would sit on his wide veranda and watch the river traffic a few hundred feet away across the lawn.

Marco Morisset built it in 1897 and named it after his wife. It had always been in the family, but since 2003, none of them came here. A management company in New Iberia sent men down to look after the house and twenty acres, and sometimes the police ran off trespassers who poked around what locals considered the closest thing to a haunted house in town. The mansion stood as a silent, lonely sentinel, holding tight to secrets about the things that happened inside its walls.

On this day, the place seemed as dark and forbidding as the stormy skies overhead. The wind whipped through the majestic oak trees and rattled the windows as the caretaker's pickup clanged over the drawbridge a quarter mile away. He was coming to be sure the place was battened down, because this storm just might become a problem for folks in these parts. You never knew, but since Craig Morisset paid a management company to take care of his house, this man would double-check every window and door — except for those three doors on the top floor that were locked. The owner's instructions were that nobody opened them, period. He'd even installed cameras in the hallway. The caretaker had no idea whether they worked, but it didn't matter. He wasn't paid to snoop, and being inside the house gave him the willies anyway. He followed the rules. Rule number one: get in, do your business and get out. Rule number two: never, ever go in there after dark. That was how he dealt with Amelia House.

This was shaping up to be a hell of a storm, and people in the area were on alert. Hurricanes Rita and Ike had devastated southern Louisiana a few years back, leaving destruction and heartache in their wakes as they tore through Acadiana. There was no way to tell if this would be the big one, where it would come ashore, or what would happen after it did. Residents had done the drill many times. For the moment they'd keep a watchful eye and wait.

Today the storm was an unnamed tropical depression in the Gulf of Mexico two hundred miles due west of Tampa. It moved northwest at sixty miles an hour, building steam as it went. Some predicted landfall near Mobile, but most trackers put it more to the northwest, coming ashore in Plaquemine or maybe Terrebonne Parish southwest of New Orleans. If it was anything like Rita in 2005, there would be mass evacuations, billions of dollars in damage, and another disruption for the hardy Cajuns, who had endured storm after storm through the years. People hoped it wouldn't be that bad as they bought water and plywood and made sure their generators were full of fuel.

Amelia House had withstood storms for over a hundred years, standing alone on high ground near the bayou. Inside, behind the locked doors, the things that waited paid no attention to storms. Nothing mattered except the return of a Morisset. Months turned into years and years into decades, and still no family member walked into the old mansion. Someday that would change, and on that day, the things would wait no more.

CHAPTER TWO

Thursday Morning

A voice came over the intercom. "Time to buckle up, Mr. M. We're cleared for takeoff."

Craig stowed his backpack under his seat, fastened the seat belt and put his head back on the plush leather seat. The Citation Encore jet taxied out, made a final turn and barreled down the runway. The pilot banked to the left, and the private airport outside Key Largo was soon far behind them. Most days they would have headed due west, crossing the state of Florida in minutes and heading out over the warm Gulf waters, but today the pilot took a different route, one that would make the trip an hour longer.

Today they had to deal with the massive tropical depression building in the Gulf two hundred miles west of Tampa. The pilot filed a flight plan that took them north around the storm. He would turn west at Tallahassee and skirt the coast across the Florida panhandle, Alabama and Mississippi, and they would arrive at the Acadiana Regional Airport in New Iberia two and a half hours from now. The airport was too small for a rental-car agency, but Craig's assistant had arranged for an Escalade through the local Cadillac dealer.

Once they reached cruising altitude, the copilot came back and offered Craig a beer. Soon he was alone again with the troubling thoughts that had plagued him for the eight weeks since he had decided to go home.

Why did I agree to do this?

The day I left for college, I promised myself I'd never set foot in that house again. For twenty years I've kept the promise, so why did I let them talk me into going back there?

People in Jeanerette think I'm someone special, just because I had an idea, started a company, and got a lucky break. What if I fall apart when I step across that threshold? What if...what if something worse happens?

That was a stupid thing to think. Something worse? What does that mean? I'm thirty-nine years old, for God's sake. I'm thirty-nine, but I can't remember things that happened at my house when I was a kid.

What is it about that house? I lived there for eighteen years. Why is there so much I've forgotten?

Talking through it in his mind, he made a decision. He wouldn't go back after all. He'd do the part he signed up for, but he wouldn't go all the way.

I told them I'd be there and I will. I'll go to my hometown, but nothing on earth can make me go home.

CHAPTER THREE

Come back home to Jeanerette for our twenty-year reunion! The email's subject line was in bold black type to ensure no one would miss it. Craig had already skipped the ten-year reunion and didn't intend to attend in the future, but he had no excuse this time. On the same weekend, he would be just forty miles away from his hometown.

Craig Morisset, a young tech multimillionaire and Jeanerette's favorite son, was on his way to Louisiana to receive an award. He'd donated ten million dollars to his alma mater, St. Anne's College in Lafayette, and the school added a technology wing to the newly renamed Morisset School of Business. A ceremony and ribbon cutting were set for the Saturday of his reunion weekend. The logistics were perfect for his first trip home since 2003, even if his heart wasn't in it.

The reunion would kick off late Friday afternoon with a tour of his old high school and an assembly in the auditorium. Afterwards they'd go to New Iberia to a restaurant for drinks, dinner and reuniting with good friends, some of whom hadn't seen each other for two decades. On Saturday morning one of his classmates who owned an old plantation home invited everyone for a tour and luncheon. Craig would miss that, since his ceremony in Lafayette began at ten, but he'd be back for the wrap-up dinner on Saturday evening at the New Iberia country club.

The only people he cared about seeing were the guys who'd been his buddies. Craig was a loner, a smart guy who did well in subjects he cared about, wasn't interested in sports or girls, and didn't have a lot of friends.

Everyone called them the Cajun Cavalry — four guys who were closer than brothers during their high school days. As friends often do upon graduation, they went in separate directions. One attended Tulane, became a doctor and lived in Atlanta. Another's parents owned a beer distributorship. He graduated from LSU, moved to Lake Charles and joined the company. The third, the quarterback of the football team, attended LSU on a scholarship, fractured his leg in a workout before the first game, and dropped out of school a month later. He jumped from job to job, struggled with depression and financial difficulty, and today he sold cars at a dealership in Metairie.

Craig's story was completely different. He went to St. Anne's University and majored in computer science. During his sophomore year, he hit the jackpot. He came up with a novel idea to offer credit monitoring and identity-theft protection to individuals, and he started KeenLock from his dorm room. Already worth millions when he graduated in 2002, in 2012 he sold his company to a Fortune 500 giant for $780 million.

These days Craig was an angel investor, identifying startup companies with possibilities. He'd invest a million here and two there, hoping to hit it big on one or two while sitting on the board of directors and giving advice and counsel to young entrepreneurs like he had been. He moved to Key Largo, Florida, bought a ninety-foot Hatteras he christened *Sassy Pants*, and kept her berthed at the exclusive Key Vista Club on the Atlantic Ocean. The five-bedroom yacht was his home, a crew of three and a personal assistant his staff, and the world his oyster.

He kept a low profile in the seven years since he sold KeenLock, and his only connection to Iberia Parish was an occasional article in the *Daily Iberian* that rehashed his accomplishments and opined if he'd ever return. "Craig Morisset could buy the whole town of Jeanerette," one writer quipped. "Amelia House sits empty, waiting for him to reclaim the Morisset throne," another said, raising the question locals asked about why he paid men to maintain the house as it was in 2003, while never returning himself.

Craig settled back in the plush seat of his nine-million-dollar private jet and closed his eyes as it banked left and headed west toward Louisiana and his childhood home.

CHAPTER FOUR

Landry Drake was in the middle of something interesting. A viewer had emailed a firsthand account of her time as a servant in the Lalaurie Mansion. Considered one of the most haunted sites in a city teeming with them, the old house stood just blocks away from Channel Nine's studio in the French Quarter.

The woman's story was fascinating. Madam Lalaurie's house, now privately owned, had been closed to the public for years, but the woman had recently worked there as a maid. The things she encountered almost daily were eerie enough to frighten the most jaded ghost hunter. Landry's computer screen brimmed with articles about the house, its cruel owner, Madam Lalaurie, and its bloody past.

Ted Carpenter, the station manager and Landry's boss, walked into his office and said, "You're from Jeanerette, right?"

Without taking his eyes off the monitor, Landry answered, "Yep. Iberia Parish born and raised."

"I have an assignment for you in Lafayette."

With a sigh of resignation, Landry stopped, swiveled his chair, and looked at Ted. "Wrong parish. This coonass is from the next one south."

"Don't worry. You'll be in Jeanerette too. You're spending the weekend."

"Jeanerette's a quiet little town. I can't imagine anything supernatural going on where I grew up."

These days Landry was a well-known TV personality, the creator and host of the popular *Bayou Hauntings* series loved by viewers everywhere. He carried the official title of investigative reporter at WCCY Television, the voice of the Crescent City, but most of his assignments involved the paranormal.

"Nothing supernatural about this one, I'm sorry to say. Sometimes even the great Landry Drake has to step down a notch. Just kidding — the truth is, I don't have anyone else to send on this one. It'll be a nice change of pace to do a human-interest piece for a change. Ever heard of Craig Morisset?"

"The tech guru? Who hasn't? I was Jeanerette's poster boy until Craig one-upped me and sold his company for a gazillion dollars."

"He gave ten million bucks to his college in Lafayette, and they built a building with his name on it. There's a ceremony in two weeks, and I want you to cover it."

"That's in Lafayette, but you said I'm going to Jeanerette too. What's that about?"

"That's the human-interest angle. I found out his twentieth high school class reunion is the same weekend. I don't know if he'll attend, but if he's coming to Lafayette anyway, I figure he'll go see his classmates."

The story meant nothing to Landry, but Ted was right. The story had a human-interest aspect. South Louisiana kid becomes one of the state's wealthiest people — that kind of thing.

THE EXPERIMENTS: THE BAYOU HAUNTING

Although ten years younger than Craig, Landry remembered a little about his parents' tragic deaths. Craig grew up in a mansion on Bayou Teche called Amelia House. His father and mother burned to death in a freak accident on the property fifteen or so years ago when Craig was away at college. After their deaths, Craig never returned to Jeanerette. The house sat empty the entire time Landry was in middle and high school. Maybe it was still vacant today. He hadn't laid eyes on it in years.

An old, empty house on a bayou, abandoned for decades. A tragic accident that claimed the parents of a teenaged entrepreneur. A troubled young man who never again set foot in his childhood home.

Landry's mind raced. *What if — what if there was something supernatural about Craig Morisset's history?*

Ted's voice jarred Landry back to reality. "Hey, hey, I see the wheels spinning. Don't make more out of this than it is. Local boy makes good, sells company, and ends up with almost a billion. Gives a chunk of change to his alma mater. That's good enough for me. I'm not sending you out on a *Bayou Hauntings* segment. This is a two-day job. Up and back. I'll email you the details."

"What about the storm?" Landry asked. "How do you know Craig Morisset will show up if the hurricane hits?"

"You know storms. It could as easily be in Alabama Saturday as here. The drive's less than three hours. Just go up there. If you get rained out, come home. No big deal."

If I have to go cover some rich guy's award, I might as well see what else I can turn up. After all, I'll be in the neighborhood.

Although this story was a human-interest assignment, Landry did the same background work as for his paranormal investigations. Interesting things often arose from the most mundane sources. He searched courthouse records and the online archives of his former employer, the *Daily Iberian* newspaper. Taken as one, obituaries, deeds of sale, news articles and other tidbits weaved a tapestry of history about families and their houses.

He spent the afternoon digging up what little he could find about Craig Morisset. He'd made the news a lot before selling his company in 2012, but after moving to Florida and buying a boat to live on, the stories stopped. He saw articles about the fire that took the lives of Frank and Maria Morisset in 2003, and he read their brief obituaries. They'd perished in a blaze that consumed an outbuilding on the grounds of Amelia House.

Before he left for the day, he thought about calling Cate, but it was eleven p.m. in London and she might be asleep. He texted instead, telling her he loved and missed her and to have a good time.

He and Cate Adams had dated long distance for several years. Their relationship was serious, but she lived in Galveston and ran her father's psychiatric practice. With two career-driven individuals, finding a way to live in the same city was a challenge they hadn't figured out yet. She'd been away a week visiting a sorority sister from LSU who worked for the London branch of a Wall Street investment bank. He and Cate met up every second or third weekend and talked almost every day, but now she was busy with her friend, and they had only spoken once since she left.

Landry walked down Royal toward Canal Street and turned in at the Monteleone Hotel. As touristy as it was, tonight he wanted to sit at the Carousel Bar, one of his and Cate's hangouts when their relationship had been new. He would toast her trip with a Sazerac and think about the good times they'd have when she returned.

Tonight his solitary drink and reverie weren't to be. The bar was packed, he couldn't get a seat on the revolving carousel, his friend the bartender was so busy Landry couldn't catch his eye, and two tourists asked for an

THE EXPERIMENTS: THE BAYOU HAUNTING 5

autograph. He gave up and walked back to his apartment on St. Philip.

CHAPTER FIVE

Although Craig Morisset's reunion didn't kick off until Friday evening, Landry drove to Iberia Parish the afternoon before. He liked to arrive early for assignments to orient himself with the area, decide what to do and in what order, and chat with the locals. Casual conversations often turned up useful information.

Landry passed through Jeanerette without stopping. There would be time to explore his hometown tomorrow morning. He planned to crash the reunion tomorrow night, be in Lafayette for the ten a.m. dedication ceremony Saturday, and head back to New Orleans afterwards.

His hands sore from gripping the wheel as he battled heavy rain and winds the entire trip, he was glad to arrive in New Iberia. He had a confirmed reservation for two nights at a bed-and-breakfast there, but tropical storms sometimes turned nasty. When that happened, people evacuated, scrambled madly for lodging, and displaced locals got rooms someone else had reserved.

The registration clerk sat in the lobby behind a beautiful antique desk. She recognized Landry and said she'd been looking forward to meeting him. He handed over his driver's license and credit card and glanced at an events calendar.

Jeanerette High School Class of 1998
Cajun Cavalry private party, 7–10 p.m.
Stonewall Jackson Room

1998 — Craig's class. He pointed to the sign and asked, "Are the people involved in that party staying here?"

"I'm not sure who's involved. Dr. Scorza is, because he's the one who rented the room." She handed Landry an old-fashioned key.

Scorza. An unusual name, one that would be easy to search.

"Is Craig Morisset staying here too?"

"Yes, he arrived an hour ago. Would you like to leave a message for him?"

Landry shook his head. The hotel only had a few rooms, and he would recognize Craig — he'd seen his picture plenty of times as he researched articles and features about the wealthiest young man in Louisiana.

The clerk reminded him his reservation was for two nights only and apologetically asked him to initial a statement that he would vacate by nine a.m. Saturday. He assured her he understood that people fleeing the approaching storm needed rooms too.

He dropped off his things in the room and found the bar tucked into an intimate corner of a long room that had once been the antebellum home's library. It had a cozy feel and Landry took a seat at the bar half an hour before the party would start. The door into the Stonewall Jackson Room was just across the hall and from where he sat he could watch the guests arrive. He planned to corner Craig long enough to ask why he hadn't come home in years.

A guy several years older than Landry came out of the Jackson Room, walked through the bar and asked the bartender to make sure they had plenty of ice all evening. The man wore white linen slacks and an untucked blue cotton shirt with rolled-up long sleeves. You couldn't miss his air of self-confident smugness as he tossed a twenty across the bar and said, "I'm counting on you, pard."

"I'll take care of it, Dr. Scorza," the bartender promised. Landry watched the man leave. He'd done a quick search a few minutes ago and knew a few things about him. He was a thirty-nine-year-old internist who graduated from Jeanerette High in 1998 and went to Tulane. He was in medical school when Katrina hit in 2005, and he treated storm victims at Charity Hospital and in the Superdome. Now practicing in Atlanta, Scorza had a wife and two children. Landry wondered if he'd brought his wife along to the reunion. He'd bet Martin had left her home with the kids.

By a quarter after seven several guests had arrived, but Craig wasn't among them. Landry wondered if he hadn't been part of the Cajun Cavalry, whatever that was.

Regardless, Landry wanted in. Everyone in the room would know something about Craig, and background information was what he needed. He watched people walk in, but he didn't remember any of them. About to give up, he got a break. Someone he knew strolled down the hall.

Bob Henry was the older brother of Tom, a classmate of Landry's. When Landry called his name, he came through the bar and gave Landry a bear hug.

"My God, man. It's great to see you! You're quite the celebrity. Thanks to your shows, my kids and I are ghost fanatics. What on earth are you doing here?"

Landry explained about the Craig Morisset connection, and Bob said the money Craig donated seemed to be all people talked about. "I work in Lafayette, and now the only thing people want is to send their kids to St. Anne's. It's a wonderful thing to do for a great little school, if you ask me."

Bob explained the event across the hall. Although the reunion festivities started tomorrow, Marty Scorza, the founder of the foursome his classmates dubbed the Cajun Cavalry, had rented the room to hold a pre-reunion cocktail party for a dozen classmates out of the fifty-five who had reservations for the weekend festivities. The invitees had once been friends; twenty years ago in high school they'd been part of the same social circle.

"Will Craig be at that party? I heard he's staying in the hotel."

"If he's staying here, then I'd say he's coming. He was one of the Cavalrymen, and those guys were closer than brothers. If he's in town, he wouldn't miss a chance to get together with them."

"Any way you can get me in there? I'd like to talk to him."

"Sure. You graduated from Jeanerette High too, even though you're a youngster compared to us old farts! That's reason enough to get you in; plus you're the famous Landry Drake! Come on!"

Bob introduced Landry to Marty Scorza, who welcomed him. "Always room for another hometown boy," he said. "Grab a drink and make yourself at home."

Landry got a beer, and several people came up to him to ask about his show and why he was there. "I loved the one you did here in Iberia Parish," one said, referring to the "Forgotten Men" episode that unfolded in a ghost town called Victory. "What brings you to our neck of the woods this time? Are there ghosts in Jeanerette too?" That elicited a laugh from the others — Jeanerette didn't seem the place for supernatural events.

"If you hear of any, tell me! Seriously, I'm here for something else entirely. I'm covering Craig Morisset's ceremony at St. Anne's on Saturday. I came a few days early to look around the old hometown and happened to pick the same B&B where your party is."

From across the room, Landry saw Craig come through the door. Marty Scorza approached him, shook his hand

THE EXPERIMENTS: THE BAYOU HAUNTING 5

and called a couple of other men over. One broke away and got Craig a mixed drink, and soon they were engrossed in conversation.

"That's what the Cajun Cavalry looks like when they've marched over the hill," Landry's friend Bob quipped. "Marty, Craig, Alain and Joe. Four brothers with different mothers. Far as I know, Craig hasn't seen the others since high school. He skipped the last reunion, and people say he hasn't been back here in years."

It seemed every guest wanted a chance to talk to Craig. They congratulated him on his success and the upcoming honor and asked how things were going. Landry positioned himself close enough to overhear in case he didn't get a chance to talk directly with him.

For a man under forty with a net worth estimated at almost eight hundred million dollars, Craig was neither a braggart nor an extrovert. He appeared embarrassed as Marty rambled on about Craig's wealth and possessions.

"I heard you're living the high life on a yacht down in Florida," Marty said as he puffed on a Cohiba cigar. "How big is it, and where all have you taken it?"

He barely paused for Craig to mumble that he had a Hatteras 90, big enough for his home and office, but nothing compared to some of the monster yachts in Key Largo. He said he didn't take it out much; it was docked most of the time, although he'd been to the Bahamas and up the east coast in recent months.

"Guess you have a crew to handle a boat that big. Three? Four? What does it take? Guess money's no object to a guy like you." He slapped Craig on the back, and Landry noticed he was already tipsy, even though the party had just begun.

"Good to see you guys," Craig said, turning away from Marty to talk with his other fellow cavalrymen. "How's life treating you all?" He kidded his friend who was in the family beer business about whether Marty got a discount on the brew for tonight's party, and he asked the car salesman if the booming national economy had been good for business. As he listened, Landry got the impression Craig was a genuine guy, a self-made individual who liked to listen to others, and who wasn't pretentious or cocky like his friend the doctor.

Landry was looking toward the Cavalrymen when Craig noticed him. "Landry? It's you, isn't it?" he said, coming over with his hand extended. "Hey, man. What an honor to see you. I'm a huge fan. I can't imagine anything more fascinating than doing what you do. You're a Jeanerette boy too, as I remember. What are you doing here?"

"The truth is I came here because of you." Landry laughed, explaining his assignment. Modest again now that the spotlight was back on him, Craig changed the subject.

"Have we ever met?" Craig asked. "I guess we both came from Jeanerette, but you're a lot younger, right? What class were you in?"

"Class of '08. I'm ten years younger. I'm sure we've met, although I don't remember it either. We had to know each other in a place as small as this, but you wouldn't have had much time for a little kid like me."

Craig laughed, and Landry asked if he might ask a few questions to avoid having to bother Craig after the ceremony in Lafayette Saturday. "It won't take long," he promised. "I know you're here to see your friends and not to endure an interview."

They sat at a table in the back. Marty tried to join them, but Craig waved him off, asking for a few minutes alone. As he often did before an interview, Landry gave Craig his cell phone number, saying he'd appreciate a call later if Craig thought of anything he wanted to add.

From the outset Craig was forthcoming and cordial, casually explaining why he hadn't been in his family home since his parents died sixteen years ago, how having so much money affected a small-town Louisiana boy, and what he was up to these days.

Craig was worth over five million dollars by the time he graduated from St. Anne's. They talked about how a twenty-one-year-old millionaire dealt with the publicity and hype, the fair-weather friends who popped up, how other kids with an idea asked for advice on starting a company when they really wanted a backer, and that not knowing who you could trust as a true friend was the loneliest part of all. It was a poignant story, and Landry appreciated Craig's allowing him to hear it.

For his part, Craig was impressed that Landry asked probing questions about him and his feelings, and not just the standard throwaways about "small-town kid hits the jackpot" that usually came up in conversation with strangers.

He said, "I started KeenLock when I was at St. Anne's in Lafayette. My parents and I weren't close — they were career-driven people — and when I went off to school, I found things that interested me. I enjoyed the classes I took, and I was glad to be away from Jeanerette, if you know what I mean. Lafayette's not that big, but it's a hell of a lot bigger than this town is. After a while I got busy with my company, and I just didn't come back. Does that make sense?"

Landry nodded.

"When my father and mother died, that was it. Between you and me, there wasn't much in that old house except bad memories. So I never went back."

Craig's face clouded for a moment, as if he had just figured something out. "Amelia House is what you came here for, right? Given what happened there and what you do, I get it. You should have told me up front. There's no way you're going inside my house."

What an odd thing to say, Landry thought as he shook his head. "That's not right, Craig. I told you the truth about why I'm here. This weekend I'm a reporter, not an investigator. I'm here to cover your ceremony at St. Anne's. But now I'm curious. Why did you bring up the house? What happened there that you think I'd be interested in?"

Craig stammered an answer, and it was obvious he wished he could take back what he'd said. "I only meant because of the fire and all. The minute I saw you I just thought..."

"Thought what? That I was here to investigate the deaths of your parents? All I know is it was a freak accident. Is there more to it than that?"

"I made an incorrect assumption, that's all. I need to wrap this up. I'm here to see my friends. Do you have one last question?"

There were lots of things, but Landry's time was over. Getting back to the human-interest part of the interview, he asked if Craig had any brothers and sisters. It was a simple question, but it seemed to confuse him. It was as if he needed to search his brain to recall if he had siblings. Landry waited, watching Craig's eyes dart about like a trapped animal looking for an escape.

Just as the silence was becoming uncomfortable, Craig muttered, "Why would you ask me that?"

What? It had been a simple question. "There was no mention of siblings in your online biography, and I wondered. Is there something wrong —"

"No! There's nothing wrong and I don't have a brother. Didn't, I mean. I didn't have a brother."

Craig stood and strode across the room to the bar. He ordered a drink, and Landry waited for his return, but Craig walked away and joined a small group.

He's not coming back. This interview is over because of something about a brother he says he doesn't have?

Landry picked up another beer and wandered the room, talking to a few people who recognized him and trying to understand what had caused Craig to act as he had.

For his part, Craig pretended to be involved in idle conversation, mostly listening as others talked, and spitting out canned answers to the same questions everyone always asked. What it was like to be at the top at a young age, what kind of toys did he own, and did he have any surefire stock market picks. He was cordial enough, but distant. His friends thought he was somewhat aloof, but actually his mind was far, far away.

My brother.

Why did he ask if there was a brother? Did someone tell him I had one?

He had no business asking that. But why does it matter? It was a simple question, so why does it bother me?

I didn't have a brother.

Did I?

CHAPTER SIX

Landry watched Craig leave the party a few minutes later. He found Marty, thanked him for allowing him to attend, and left too. His work was done for tonight.

He walked up to his room on the second floor and realized that the party venue lay just below him. In the room he hadn't noticed the noise, but now through the floor he heard muted conversations, the thump-thumping of the bass tones from the music, and the sporadic guffaws of one inebriated classmate or another. It surprised him how much noise twelve people made, but he blamed it on the free-flowing booze, which made folks both chatty and loud.

The noise from downstairs wasn't the only issue. The storm had intensified, whipping tree limbs and scratching at his room's windowpanes. He looked outside and saw sheets of rain that created huge pools of water in the broad expanse of lawn below. He pulled up a weather app and found things had changed while he had been downstairs. Now a Category 2 hurricane named George, sat less than two hundred miles southeast of the Louisiana coast. As it drifted northwest towards Plaquemine Parish, residents of Pilottown, Grand Isle and Port Fourchon had received evacuation orders, and those in delta towns to the north and west might face the same by morning.

As he wrote notes about his discussion with Craig, he considered himself fortunate to have saved the question about siblings for last. By the time the odd guy had walked away, he had plenty of background to use in his story.

He wondered about the incident involving the house. Craig was aggressive in his insistence Landry couldn't go inside, even though Landry hadn't brought it up. He had done hundreds of interviews, and if there was ever a subject with something to hide, it was Craig Morisset.

He'd deal with that later. Thankful he'd brought along noise-cancelling headphones, Landry put them on, climbed into bed, and fell asleep.

Something woke Craig. Did he hear a door slam? Or someone shouting? Something — but now there was nothing, not a sound except the wailing of the wind.

Where am I?

He raised his head and realized he was lying on a couch, wearing the same clothes that now were soaked. The room was so dark that he couldn't see a thing. Shaking his head to clear the cobwebs, he struggled to remember where he was.

Realities formed in his mind. The B&B. The reunion party. The reporter Landry Drake. The repetitious questions from classmates he hadn't seen in years. Slipping away early. Walking up the stairs and going into his room.

Where am I? My room didn't have a couch. Why am I not in bed, and why are my clothes drenched?

He stood, stretched out his arms, and walked around trying to find a wall and a light switch. After a few steps he hit something solid — a large piece of furniture — maybe an armoire.

THE EXPERIMENTS: THE BAYOU HAUNTING 5

There wasn't an armoire in my room. Where the hell am I?

He slammed into a wall and felt his way along it to avoid running into something else. He found a door frame but no light switch. He moved to the other side, and at last his fingers closed around it. A little worried about what he'd see, he switched it on.

An old chandelier hung in the center of a bedroom, its few working bulbs creating a shadowy half-light.

Something was wrong. Very, very wrong.

Craig knew this place — this room — but he couldn't retrieve the memory from the recesses of his mind. This wasn't the hotel. This was a place captured in time, a bedroom waiting for someone to return. He saw the covers neatly turned down, the pillows fluffed, and a stack of wood near a massive fireplace in case the night turned cool.

A low rumble of thunder reminded him why he was soaked. There was a hurricane coming. It was pouring, and he must have been out in it.

He walked to a nightstand next to the beautiful four-poster bed he remembered from sometime long ago, and he picked up a notecard lying there. He recognized the handwriting in an instant. Tears streamed down his cheeks as he realized where he was, although he didn't know why or how he got here.

Welcome to Amelia House, the card said, in handwriting with beautiful swirly flourishes his mother used for formal occasions.

This was Amelia House — *his* house — and he was in one of the second-floor guest bedrooms. His mother always left a note by the beds to welcome guests. This card had been on the nightstand since the last guest left maybe twenty years ago. No one had visited since.

Not even Craig.

Only the people he hired to maintain the place had been in this house.

BILL THOMPSON

Wiping his eyes with his sleeve, he opened the door and stepped out into the hallway. The house was dark, but dim light filtered through the windows over the staircase, and the swaying branches cast skeleton-like shadows on the walls.

Craig went to the far end of the hall and turned on the lights. The matching chandeliers were in good working order, flooding the hallway with light. All the doors on this floor were open, just as Mother always insisted they be. The ones upstairs were a different story. For a second, he wondered what would happen if he went upstairs, walked halfway along the hall, and knocked on her bedroom door. Would she invite him in, as she always did?

He dared not go there. Instead, he checked his watch and saw it was a quarter past three on Friday morning. He had left the party five hours ago and gone straight up to his room. How did he get from New Iberia to Jeanerette — twelve miles — without remembering the drive? Alcohol wasn't the culprit; he'd had only a couple of gin and tonics all evening.

It was something else.

I drove here. I must have done that, but how could I navigate the highway and not remember? He took the stairs to the ground floor, passed one familiar room after another, and flipped on the lights. He tried the massive oaken front door his great-grandfather had imported from France.

It's locked tight, so how did I get in? I don't have a key. I haven't had a key in seventeen years.

He unlocked the door and opened it. The force of the storm blew the door toward him, striking him on the arm. He cried out and his voice echoed through the old house. Another memory. As a child, his mother showed him how you could whisper at the front door and hear it in the back kitchen. Something her grandfather created when he built the house, she revealed. *A secret thing, just between us. Don't tell your brother.*

THE EXPERIMENTS: THE BAYOU HAUNTING 5

My brother? That's not what she said. It couldn't have been, because I don't have a brother. Why did I think that?

She said, "Don't tell your father." That's what she said.

He locked the door and turned, taking in the long hallway that ran from one end of the house to the other. Many old mansions in the South had this layout, designed to capture the breezes and keep the house cool. This house was built in 1897, long after the war, by Marco Morisset, a self-taught physician who emigrated from France. He named it Amelia House after his wife, who ran the household and sugar cane plantation with a staff of freedmen and women.

Another door — the back door — stood at the opposite end of the hall, and he remembered that's how he came inside. He walked to it, found it unlocked, and inched it open. In the raging storm he saw the rental car parked by the porch.

I drove here. Or sleep-drove. Like sleepwalking but a million times more dangerous. Driving under the influence of...slumber.

He walked from room to room, recalling this piece of furniture and that. He tinkled the keys of the piano his grandfather had bought in 1949 in Boston and had shipped by boat to New Orleans. The off-key thuds reminded him he needed to hire a piano tuner.

No I don't, because I don't live here. No one does. Who cares if the piano's tuned? Why do I even pay people to maintain this place? Why can't I just sell it and be done? Nothing's stopping me.

Nothing but...

A rush of cold air swept through the room and enveloped him. He shuddered and wrapped his arms around his body.

I can't get rid of the house because of...something.
What is it?
Mother, what is it? What's the secret?

CHAPTER SEVEN

Friday Morning

At seven, Landry stood outside the door and waited for the breakfast room to open. He wanted to get a cup of coffee and go back upstairs to shower and prepare for the day. He didn't expect to run into other guests, because he figured last night's party must have run until the wee hours.

The TV was tuned to a Baton Rouge station, and a weatherman predicted Hurricane George would make landfall in Terrebonne Parish around noon as a Category 2 storm. Landry glanced out the window. Here, eighty miles north of the Gulf, the rain had eased a little, but water pooled in the parking lot and street. On the highway out front, a long line of headlights moved slowly north, residents obeying the governor's mandatory evacuation of coastal parishes. Landry knew many others would hunker down in place. They'd ridden out storms before, and this time they'd do it again. He just hoped no one got hurt; sometimes things turned very bad after it was too late to evacuate.

The last person he expected to see up this early met him in the breakfast room and slapped him on the back. Marty looked like twenty miles of bad road — bloodshot eyes, puffy lids and breath that smelled like a brewery. Landry hadn't shaved yet, but Marty's rough stubble added credence to the idea that the doctor was experiencing a major hangover.

He was livelier than Landry would have expected. "Hey, buddy! You're the youngster in the crowd, but you punked out early last night! What happened to you?"

"Long day, I guess. Everything caught up to me. What time did your ten p.m. party shut down?"

"I don't know. One thirty, maybe two." After looking for a server, he began opening cabinet doors.

"The coffee's over there —"

"This isn't a coffee morning," he said with a grin. He walked across the hall to the party room and came back with a half-empty fifth of Smirnoff. "Now I wonder where they keep the tomato juice." He found a pitcher on the buffet, put ice in a tall glass, and filled it with vodka. He added a splash of juice, squeezed in a wedge of lemon, and took a long drink.

Landry excused himself, saying he was heading to Jeanerette today to look around his old hometown. Marty said, "If you're staying over, why don't you join us for the reunion parties tonight?" He said they'd meet at the high school for an assembly at five p.m. and come back to a restaurant here in New Iberia for cocktails and dinner.

What a break! Funny how the world works. This guy may be obnoxious, but thanks to him I don't have to crash parties to get close to Craig. He thanked Marty, said he'd be there, left the room, and walked across the lobby to the stairs.

Just then Craig walked through the front door, looking like he'd spent the night outdoors. He was soaked through, matted hair hung down his forehead, and he seemed disoriented.

Landry said, "Craig, are you okay?"

Craig held up his hands and told Landry to leave him alone. He slogged through the lobby, leaving a trail of wet footprints across a beautiful old rug, and trudged up the stairway.

Landry went to his room too. He saw a black Escalade in the parking lot that hadn't been there earlier, which he presumed was Craig's.

The hot shower hit the spot. Back downstairs, he filled his YETI tumbler with coffee and donned a rain jacket. He drove to the highway and waited. Northbound traffic was still solid, but soon a courteous driver let him cross over to the other side. Thinking Old Jeanerette Road would have less traffic, he went across the Teche on the Olivier Road drawbridge. He'd never seen the water this high, and he wondered if the authorities would close the bridge.

His phone buzzed with a weather advisory. George was a Category 3 now, churning up water fifteen miles south of Cocodrie, a tiny shrimp and crabbing town on the coast in Terrebonne Parish. Warnings were issued for inland parishes like Iberia, whose residents might be ordered to evacuate soon.

Growing up here, Landry had ridden out many storms. His parents believed in hunkering down instead of leaving their property behind for who knew how long. Hurricane George would weaken once it made landfall — they always did — but he knew the double punch of gale-force winds and torrential rain could still cause significant problems to whatever areas it struck.

He drove into Jeanerette and crossed back over the Teche on the Bayside drawbridge to get to the house where he grew up. Only twelve miles south of New Iberia, the swollen river ran fiercely downstream, battering boats tied up along the shore. He let a call from an unknown number go to voicemail and then listened. It was the hotel clerk reminding him of tomorrow's nine a.m. mandatory checkout. He wasn't surprised; every room for miles around was rented by now. If Hurricane George maintained its speed, the worst would be over by tomorrow afternoon and he could drive back to New Orleans. It might be raining cats and dogs, but he'd get home.

If things didn't go so well, then he'd have to decide where to weather the storm. Unless they cancelled the reunion events, everyone else who stayed faced the same issue, so he'd ask when he returned that afternoon. Craig's ceremony at St. Anne's University was set for ten tomorrow morning, and Landry figured they'd postpone it. Although it was almost an hour's drive north, Lafayette was still in the storm's currently projected path.

He found an open gas station and decided to fill up while he could. A quick call to the university confirmed that the Saturday event was off. The dedication would be two weeks later, which for Landry meant another trip for a story he hadn't wanted to cover in the first place.

He turned down the street where he grew up and noticed how much the neighborhood had deteriorated. Arriving at his house, he almost cried. It was a small place with two bedrooms and one bath, but growing up it hadn't seemed as tiny as it did now.

His parents were working people with hardly enough money to survive, but with fierce Cajun pride his mother kept up their property until Landry's father died and the money ran out. Back then there had been flowers, freshly mowed grass, paint on the house and the carport, and not even a stray baseball left overnight in the yard. As he pulled up in front and cut the engine, he noticed the difference today. He was glad his mother lived in North Carolina with her sister. It would have pained her immensely to see this, as it did him.

A car sat on blocks in the front yard, and a drenched pit bull chained to a metal stake barked and lunged toward Landry. Dozens of broken toys, a discarded clothes washer and a pirogue with a hole in its side littered the property. The screen door opened and a man in a sleeveless undershirt stepped around a doorless refrigerator, cursed at the dog, and finally noticed Landry's Jeep. He strode across his yard, and Landry rolled down his car window.

"What do you want?"

"I lived here ten years ago. I was in town and I stopped by to see how it looked."

"You're Landry Drake, ain't ya? Me and the wife seen your TV shows. I know you used to live here. Well, it ain't no palace, but it wasn't when your folks was here either, I reckon. They was poor as hell, far as I heard." He snorted a half-grunt, half-laugh.

"I'll go now. I feel sorry for your dog. If he doesn't stop straining on his chain, he's going to hurt himself."

"Won't be the first time," the slovenly man replied. "Don't feel sorry for him. He ain't your dog." He walked through the yard, kicked at the animal as he passed, and went inside.

CHAPTER EIGHT

Landry drove a block to Main Street and found a sea of northbound cars fleeing the storm a hundred miles to the south. The rain was coming down steadily, and every headlight was on against thick low-hanging clouds and high humidity that made the morning as dark as night. He saw plywood sheets covering store windows, and gusts of wind whipped up dirt and debris in whirling mini-tornadoes. Almost everything in town was closed up tight, but he knew a place he'd bet was open, an oasis with coffee and donuts for weary travelers. A mile down the highway he turned in to Coach's Corner, its red neon letters piercing the gloom like an inviting beacon. The plate-glass windows were boarded up, but a sign above the entrance flashed O-P-E-N.

I knew it. He'd have been amazed if Coach Walker had evacuated. He found a parking spot in the crowded lot and went inside.

The air was warm and steamy, and the line of people seemed mesmerized by the tantalizing aroma of freshly baked donuts and steaming-hot coffee. Kids pointed to trays in glass showcases, choosing pink sprinkles or chocolate glazed or a dozen holes. Behind the counter a matronly woman in her sixties filled orders and tended a huge coffee pot. Through a serving window behind her, Landry saw Cal Walker, his high school basketball coach, transfer a tray of glazed bear claws from the oven to the counter.

"Order up, honey," the man said, and his wife moved the tray to a case. Coach looked out at the line of customers and waved to several people. Today many of his patrons were strangers from south of Jeanerette, but there were locals too, and Coach knew them all.

Landry waved and Coach gave him a big smile. He came out through a swinging door, wiped his hands on his sugar-coated apron, and motioned Landry to come behind the counter.

"Hey, big guy! It's good to see you. What the hell are you doing in town in the middle of a hurricane? That TV station got you doing the weather now?"

"No, thank God. It's bad enough I'm doing a story on Craig Morisset when I ought to be ghost-hunting, don't you think?"

Coach nodded and said, "Wish I could sit and talk, but we gotta take care of these folks until the supplies run out. I figured if I'm not leaving, I might as well feed people on the road. If you've got a few minutes, come in the back and lend a hand. I could use the help."

Soon Landry was outfitted in a hairnet, apron and rubber gloves, and he followed Coach's orders, just like in high school basketball practice. He'd never made donuts before, but it didn't take long to get the hang of it. He smiled and waved when customers who looked through the serving window pointed at the famous paranormal investigator who was Coach's kitchen assistant.

Two exhausting hours later it was over. Coach ran out of flour and eggs, and the coffee pot was almost empty. He served a few more customers, turned off his signs, and stuck his head outside as the last people left. "Wall-to-wall cars going north out there," he commented as he came in and locked the door. "Rain's picking up again too. This is going to get nasty."

He fetched three cups of steaming black coffee, joined his wife and Landry at a table, and switched on a TV hanging in a corner. Hot and sweaty from the close quarters and the oven, Landry removed his gloves, hairnet and apron and wiped his brow with his sleeve. He stretched his aching back and watched a Lafayette weatherman show George's expected path. With sustained winds over sixty miles an hour, it had slowed as it moved toward the coast. The most recent track showed it making landfall at Cocodrie, passing over Morgan City tonight and then moving up through St. Martin Parish east of Jeanerette. The forecaster predicted eight to ten more inches of rain for their area, but warned if the storm stalled out, there would be a lot more.

Coach watched the weather for a moment and walked to the kitchen. "I saved a few donuts from the last batch. Momma, I'll bring us a couple. How about you, Landry?"

They laughed when Landry declined, saying he didn't think he'd ever eat another donut. They were accustomed to hours of constant work prepping one batch of pastry after another, handling a nonstop flow of customers, many of whom were noisy toddlers, and taking no rest breaks until the food ran out. They thought nothing of eating a donut after hours of slinging dough to make them, even though the very thought of one turned Landry's stomach.

Coach thanked him for pitching in, saying they couldn't have handled the crowd without him. Then he asked what the hell Landry was doing in Jeanerette. Was he crazy? Didn't he know a hurricane was coming? Laughing, Landry assured them he had made an informed decision to stay and explained why he'd come to Iberia Parish.

"That Morisset boy did well, didn't he?" Mrs. Walker said. "He was several years ahead of you, as I recall."

Ten, Landry replied, and Coach Walker mentioned that he'd retired the year after Landry graduated in 2008. "I sat around the house for almost a year before buying the donut shop. About drove me crazy doing nothing," he admitted, and his wife said he wasn't the only one. It about drove her crazy too.

"Now he gets to come down here every morning and hang out with his friends. On weekends a part-time high school girl helps out behind the counter, so I'm not tied to this place like Coach is. He can hang out here in his own element. It's never as hectic as today, thank God." She tapped her husband lightly on the arm. "I imagine you'd sell the place if you had to work this hard every day!"

Landry commented on how contented and healthy they both appeared to be, and switched the conversation back to Craig. He sometimes asked questions to which he knew the answers, seeing what new information he might learn.

"Does he come home often?"

"Never, from what I hear," Coach said. "People say he hasn't been back since his folks died in that fire."

"Where are they buried?"

"Boy, you've been gone too long! Don't you remember the Morisset crypt in St. John the Evangelist Cemetery? You had to have seen it when you were a kid — everyone did. It's hard to miss, since it's the biggest one in the entire graveyard. All the Morissets are buried in there, all the way back to Marco, the one who built Amelia House."

Although his present job involved lots of graveyards, back when Landry was a kid, he had never set foot in that cemetery. There had been no reason. Despite never being there, he recalled the crypt. It was so big you could see it from blocks away. His own parents, who were apparently no fans of the Morissets, once remarked that the family couldn't resist showing off how wealthy they were, even when they buried their dead.

"Do you remember his having a brother? I asked him last night, and it seemed to spook him somehow."

"What did he tell you?"

"He said no, and why did I ask."

"Well, I don't recall him having a brother. Why? Do you think he did?"

"I don't remember one, but Craig acted really strange, like I'd stumbled on a secret."

"I'm not one to repeat rumors," Coach said, which elicited a snort and a roll of the eyes from his wife. "People whisper stuff around town. You know that — you grew up here. Folks sometimes get into someone else's business. Amelia House still has all its furniture and everything else, just like it was the day the Morissets died. Even the beds are made up like someone's coming tonight to sleep there. One of the maintenance guys told me that. Spooky, don't you think?

"Tommy Freeman down at the real estate office told me that Amelia House will never sell. That's why Craig never put it on the market. Bad stuff happened in there. Craig's ancestors were so-called doctors, even though none of them ever darkened the door of a medical school. They did experiments on animals and people, some say. His parents did too, far as I've heard."

Mrs. Walker interrupted. "Cal, you have no business saying stuff like that. Tommy Freeman's an old busybody. You're repeating rumors, just like you said you wouldn't. The Morissets were different, that's all."

"I'll say. Craig's parents were damned strange people. If anybody in town had somebody locked up in the basement, it'd be them. If houses around here had basements, that is." He chuckled.

"That's enough. You stop that kind of talk right now! It's not right to talk disrespectfully of the dead."

"Okay, Momma." He laughed. "Whatever you say." He leaned toward Landry and stage-whispered, "Catch me later and I'll tell you more!"

It was time for him to go. Landry thanked them for the hospitality and said how much he enjoyed his morning in the kitchen. It had been good to see his old friend, and he hoped to run into Coach again before the weekend was over. He wanted to hear more rumors, because sometimes they turned out not to be rumors at all.

CHAPTER NINE

Landry told his friends goodbye and waded through the now-empty parking lot to his Jeep. The rain seemed lighter right now, but ominous storm clouds foretold what lay ahead. Even at noon the skies were so dark that the streetlights in Jeanerette were lit.

After hearing Coach talk about the mausoleum, he wanted to visit it. He drove three blocks to the cemetery and parked by the gate next to Craig's black Escalade. A hundred feet away, the Morisset mausoleum loomed above all the others, its white marble gleaming against the low clouds. Craig stood in front of it with his back to Landry.

Landry raised the hood on his windbreaker, grabbed his umbrella, tramped through the wet grass, and wove through a necropolis of aboveground crypts. Craig could easily have seen him, but he seemed transfixed, staring at the wall of names etched in marble, and talking. Through the wailing wind, his words sounded like eerie whispers, disjointed parts of a two-way conversation Landry could only hear half of.

I came here because I refuse to go where you really are.

Why did you do it? Why wouldn't you leave us alone? It wasn't fair.

Landry moved closer and Craig turned. His face was devoid of expression, and he looked at Landry through empty eyes.

"Want this?" Landry said, offering the umbrella. "You're soaked."

He said nothing.

Landry held out the umbrella, but Craig stepped backwards and murmured, "You don't belong here. This isn't a place for the living."

"These are your people. Would you tell me about them?"

Craig's lips grimaced into what might have been a smile, and he answered in a hollow, computerlike monotone. "*My people?* These are not *my people.* Not after everything that happened. They are my ancestors. Nothing more."

Landry didn't press him for answers. Landry pointed to two names on the marble slab. Francois Morisset and Maria Morisset. Two people who died on the same day in 2003, and the most recent dates on the marble markers.

"Your parents?"

Craig stared at the names as if seeing them for the first time. "Parents? That's a word that implies responsibility and love and empathy. I refer to them as parents sometimes, but that's a lie. Those two people birthed me."

"What's going on, Craig?"

Craig pointed to the right side of the mausoleum, where blank pieces of marble covered unused burial spots. "Perhaps one of those is for me. I don't have a brother, so I don't know who the others are for."

The brother again. Why does he keep saying he doesn't have a brother?

Landry said, "Someone built the mausoleum years ago. They couldn't have known how big the family would be, right? They just added extra spaces. Not just for you. For anyone else who came along over the years."

"You have no idea what they knew."

And then things changed. He turned to Landry, and the veil that masked his face was gone. He blinked his eyes and looked confused. "What are you doing here?"

Again Landry offered his umbrella, but Craig declined, saying a little more water wouldn't hurt. Without asking, Landry took out his phone and snapped pictures of the crypt and each inscription while Craig watched without emotion.

"Why did you come?"

"I visited with Coach Walker this morning. I'm building background for the story about your gift to the university, and he reminded me about your family's mausoleum. I wanted to look at it."

"How long have you been standing here?"

"A few minutes. I was worried about you. You didn't seem to realize I'd come."

"Did I — what did I say?"

Landry chose his words carefully, because he wanted to find out more about what Craig had said. "You were talking to yourself, saying they weren't family, just your ancestors. You said they made things worse by what they did."

Craig gazed at the mausoleum, and Landry asked again if he would talk about the people buried here.

He seemed to think about the request for a while, and at last he said, "If I must. Let's get it over with."

The mausoleum was huge — three rows, each with six burial spaces. Along the top ran an engraved marble slab bearing the family name Morisset. On the row just below it he saw three marble faceplates marking the resting places of Marco, Amelia and Baby Girl Morisset. The faceplates for the other three crypts on that row were blank.

"My great-grandfather and his wife," Craig said as he pointed to them. "They emigrated from France in the 1800s and built Amelia House. I guess they had a stillborn child. Nobody ever spoke of her. He built the mausoleum in the early years of the twentieth century."

He pointed to the next row, where Albert Morisset was interred next to his wife, Genevieve. The other four crypts in that row were empty too.

"My grandfather Albert. Like his own father, the human brain fascinated him. Bizarre, don't you think? He made the mistake of publishing articles about experiments and tests he performed. Real doctors at the time thought he was crazy."

Craig's words about his grandfather sounded bitter and spiteful. Landry figured Craig would have been around four years old when the man died, too young to harbor such feelings. His emotions must have arisen from things he heard about his grandfather later in life.

Landry knew what Craig meant when he said his grandfather's colleagues rebuked him. He'd read a 1975 article from the Baton Rouge newspaper. A medical review board revoked Albert's license after he distributed papers with very unconventional theories about brain surgery. Albert denied ever performing one himself, and the review board's findings were never made public, but the tone of the article indicated that the local medical community had purged itself of a pest when it stopped Albert Morisset.

Craig's father's crypt lay on the next row. Francois — nicknamed Frank — occupied the first crypt on the bottom row next to his wife, Maria. Craig passed over both without saying a word. Like the other rows, there were empty spaces.

"Your great-grandfather built a large mausoleum," Landry said. "There are more empty crypts than occupied ones. Did you have other family members who were buried somewhere else?"

THE EXPERIMENTS: THE BAYOU HAUNTING 5

"You ask too many questions. My family's business is none of yours."

Craig's overreaction to a simple comment surprised Landry. Once again, his reluctance to talk about seemingly mundane things only made Landry more curious.

On the last crypt — the bottommost right one — a word was scrawled on the blank faceplate. It looked as though someone had marked it with a piece of charcoal or a stick. Landry bent down to look and started to clear away a bit of rain-streaked dirt.

"Get away from there!"

Startled, Landry lost his balance and fell in the mud.

Craig offered him a hand and apologized for his outburst.

"What the hell was that about?" Landry blurted, wiping mud from his jeans.

"I'm sorry. I…I didn't know what you were doing."

"There's something written on the marble. It looks like a word. Look right there."

"It's nothing. It's just dirt."

"No, it's not. It looks like a short word — maybe there's a *J*. Look here." He started to crouch in front of the marker.

Craig grabbed his arm and jerked him back. "I told you to get away from there. You need to leave now."

Puzzled, Landry said goodbye and walked towards the Jeep. Halfway there he turned back and saw Craig kneeling before the marker. Landry knew he was erasing that word.

He scrolled through the photos he'd taken. He had a good shot of the bottom row, and he enlarged it, zeroing in on the blank tile. Through the encrusted dirt there was a word — not etched in marble but scrawled by hand.

A single word.

A name.

Jerry.

CHAPTER TEN

Amelia House was only two miles from the cemetery. A beautiful plantation home originally surrounded by two hundred acres, it was a showplace befitting a family of means. It was on one side of the Teche, Landry thought, while his house and the rest of town was on the other.

Landry had read the history. Marco Morisset and his wife, Amelia, emigrated from France to New Orleans in the late 1880s. A self-taught physician who traveled from town to town treating patients, he moved in 1897 to a new town called Jeanerette and bought property along Bayou Teche. There he and Amelia built what an article called "a spectacular mansion, the largest in the area, and one that's the envy of every family in Iberia Parish."

With eight thousand square feet and sporting broad shaded verandas, Amelia House was indeed a breathtaking mansion. A circular staircase built of cypress ran from the ground floor to the third. Choosing that wood had been an expensive decision; cypress was strong and termite resistant, and to force it into curves for the banister, each piece had been carefully bent and molded underwater for over a year.

After Craig's strange behavior in the cemetery, Landry knew he couldn't leave without seeing the house. He crossed over the bridge and drove until he came to a no-trespassing sign. He ignored it and turned down a lane that led to the back side of the house. The front — the beautiful side with massive Greek-revival columns and porches that ran the length of the house on two floors — faced Bayou Teche. Cool breezes came off the river, and that was where the traffic was in the days before automobiles. The back side that faced Old Jeanerette Road would have overlooked a vast sugar cane plantation in the 1800s. Even with only twenty acres left of the property today, the place remained a beautiful setting.

He parked, raised his umbrella, and ran to the back porch. Through tall windows he could see furniture in a darkened room.

He knocked on the door once, then again, turned the knob, and stepped back in surprise as the door silently swung open. *Why isn't it locked?* Nobody in Jeanerette had locked their doors when he was a kid, but that was twenty years ago. The world was different now, and this fully furnished mansion was some distance from both the road and the closest neighbor.

It's raining like crazy, I'm standing here alone, and the door's open. It's like I'm meant to go inside.

Segueing from an explainable charge of trespassing on private property to felony unlawful entry, he stepped inside and closed the door. Reminding himself he was here to get more background for his article, he stamped his wet shoes on a doormat and walked down the hall.

As Coach had said, every room was full of furniture, with knickknacks on end tables and place settings on a beautiful antique dining table. It seemed as if the owners had stepped out and would return soon, although if the stories were true, no Morisset had been here for years. The place was surreal, eerie and more than a little disconcerting.

THE EXPERIMENTS: THE BAYOU HAUNTING 5

Landry climbed the stairs and found a long hallway on the second floor. He looked through open doors into what looked like guest bedrooms. Along the far wall of each was a set of French double doors that opened onto the upstairs porch. Although the low-lying clouds and rain created poor visibility, he knew Bayou Teche lay a few hundred feet away. He climbed the stairs to the top floor and found more bedrooms on one side of the hall. Three locked rooms were on the other.

A muffled noise came from somewhere below.

"Hello?" Landry yelled. "Is someone there?"

There were odd creaking sounds like gears turning on an ancient machine. He tried to determine where the sound was coming from, and thought something might be moving inside the walls.

Given that he was at best an uninvited guest, he decided to go back downstairs. If someone had come in, he should present himself before someone with a shotgun confronted him. He found everything as he had left it, except for a second set of wet shoe prints that led from the back door down the hallway.

Someone else had come inside the house. He looked through the narrow windows that flanked the back door. Now Craig's Escalade sat next to the Jeep.

"Craig! Craig, it's me, Landry!" He paused but heard no response, so he followed the prints all the way down the hall and almost to the front door. At that point they veered into a room on the right. He stepped into a richly furnished, dark-paneled office with an enormous old Persian rug on the floor. Bookshelves lined the walls. There must have been hundreds of volumes interspersed with mementos and keepsakes. An antique desk and chair stood to one side, and in front of a fireplace sat an overstuffed leather armchair that had seen plenty of use. On a table next to it, an ashtray held a pipe. A gold lighter and a tobacco pouch lay nearby, waiting for the gentleman of the house to have a smoke and enjoy the fire.

He read book titles as he walked around the magnificent room. There were dozens of thick leather-bound medical treatises on subjects like neurology, diseases of the spine, otolaryngology, and the treatment of gastrointestinal issues. He saw bound copies of the *Journal of the American Medical Association*, the *Journal of Neurology*, and other medical magazines that dated to the early decades of the twentieth century. As self-taught physicians, Craig's grandfather and great-grandfather had spent decades accumulating and studying all these materials.

He saw many other books, some very old, with subjects as broad in scope and curious as narcolepsy, leukotomy, necrophilia, dementia praecox and trepanation. Landry knew what a few of the words meant, but most were medical terms unfamiliar to him.

Two well-worn books were almost in tatters. They were *Mental Maladies: A Treatise on Insanity* and *A History of Mental Disorders: 1900-1965*. It appeared that those volumes had seen a lot of use over the years.

There was a sepia photograph of the house dated 1898, the year after it was built. A man and woman in fancy dress stood on the front porch, and in front of them was a lineup of working-class males and females. They might have been people who built the house, but more likely they were the staff.

There were certificates evidencing Albert's attendance at medical seminars, unusual old surgical instruments that someone considered keepsakes, and a photograph of a woman with a young boy clinging to her skirt. Behind her in the shadows there was another hazy figure, perhaps a servant who hadn't intended to be caught in the photo.

"I see you've found the sanctuary."

THE EXPERIMENTS: THE BAYOU HAUNTING 5

"Damn!" Landry exclaimed. He wheeled about and saw Craig standing in a dark corner.

How did he get in here without my hearing him?

"You surprised me. I'm sorry. I didn't mean to intrude —"

In the same dull voice he said, "But you did intrude, because here you are."

Then he repeated the words he'd said at the cemetery. "This place isn't for the living."

"But this is your house. This is where you grew up."

He pondered that for a moment. "That's all it is — a place where I grew up. There was no love in this house. Only ruthless ambition. An insatiable lust for peer approval. A drive to prove their bizarre theories. You shouldn't have come here."

"I'm truly sorry, Craig."

The figure in the corner stared at Landry as though the name was unfamiliar to him. In the dim light and with the room so filled with shadows, it was impossible to see his face.

A tense feeling of unease crept up Landry's spine.

It is Craig...right? It has to be him.

Who else could it be? The guy's just acting strange, like always.

Telling himself to stop worrying, Landry turned to the medical books behind him and pointed to a few volumes. "So many of these books are about neurology and psychology. Those must have been your ancestors' specialties. I know some were doctors; was your father a physician too?"

There was no answer.

He turned around.

The figure — Craig — had vanished.

He would have had to walk thirteen feet across a hardwood floor in order to reach the hall door and the room's only exit. It would have been impossible not to hear him, but Landry had been talking about the books instead of paying attention to the person behind him.

He examined the place where Craig had stood, running his hands over the dark-stained wood panels that met at the corner. Thinking there might be a hollow space, he knocked each piece. The twelve-foot-by-four-foot rectangular panels were outlined in quarter-inch trim, and there was nothing unusual about them. He knelt and felt the dark wood flooring, but again there was nothing out of the ordinary. There were bookshelves next to the corner panels, and he peered closely at them. He'd seen shelves that moved, most recently in an old mansion called Beau Rivage that appeared in "Callie," one of Landry's *Bayou Hauntings* episodes.

He moved his fingertips up and down along the trim work and under the shelves, searching for a trip mechanism or another way a person could slip behind them. They seemed unexceptional too, although he knew that many mansions in the bayou parishes contained architectural secrets. On just the short stretch of River Road between Destrehan and White Castle, Landry had visited houses with hidden stairways, secret chambers, sliding panels that opened to crawl spaces between rooms, and doors that opened to reveal blank walls. Sometimes the reasons for including them in a house were easy to explain, but more often, they were a mystery.

Landry went from floor to floor calling Craig's name. At last he gave up, walked out the back door and just before he closed it, he heard something — that same muffled sound from upstairs — a noise like gears turning. He listened, but now there was nothing but the loud splats of raindrops on the porch.

The Escalade was still there, and so Craig was somewhere in the house. Landry couldn't imagine what had caused his odd behavior. It was none of his business, but in

THE EXPERIMENTS: THE BAYOU HAUNTING 5

his line of work, things that made no sense were the most interesting of all.

CHAPTER ELEVEN

Friday Evening

Fifty-five people had sent in reservations to attend the reunion, but on Friday afternoon only nineteen came to the Jeanerette High School auditorium. The rest — the cautious, or perhaps the smart ones — had hunkered down somewhere safe. Growing up in Iberia Parish, these folks had learned not to trust hurricanes.

Maybe George wouldn't move in this direction, or it wouldn't be as strong as the forecasters predicted. Perhaps it would fall apart completely. Or then again, it just might tear the hell out of everything, flood homes and streets, knock out the power, and leave visitors stranded for days. For many former classmates, attending a twentieth reunion wasn't worth the risk.

The ones at the high school Friday afternoon were the diehards. They came to party, see their old friends, and have a good time, and no hurricane was going to stop them. Whether they liked it or not, at this point they were stuck, because the evacuation had ended. People from the coast had already passed through. Behind them the National

Guard would close roads, keeping foolhardy storm chasers away from the coast. People who decided to stay behind — people like themselves — had to ride it out now. Emergency services and soldiers would move on to other storm-related duties. The diehards would be on their own until George passed them by.

The grads, Landry and a few teachers from those days took seats at the front of the auditorium. A dozen phones pinged at once with a storm update. In Jeanerette, over three inches of rain had fallen in the past hour, and the rainfall was much heavier to the south, where Hurricane George moved along through Terrebonne Parish.

Their moods were lighthearted. As one would expect, a few people had concerns, nervously recalling Rita or Ike or Gustav and the damage caused by those hurricanes. But most storms ended up being simply an inconvenience of greater or lesser proportion. If this storm behaved, the heavy rain should be past them in seventy-two hours. If not, they were in for the duration, and they would deal with whatever nature tossed their way.

The class president welcomed the assemblage, and someone played the piano while a cheerleader led them in the school fight song. Four teachers related memories, funny events and embarrassing moments. Landry knew them all — they'd been his teachers too. After a tour of the building and lots of reminiscing about whose lockers were where, who kissed in the hall and sneaked a smoke in the girl's bathroom, it was time to head to a restaurant back in New Iberia for drinks and dinner.

There had been lots of driving back and forth, but there was a reason. Jeanerette was too small to house and feed a large group of attendees, so the people planning the reunion months before had scheduled events both in their hometown and in New Iberia a few miles up the road. They couldn't have known there would be a hurricane that brought flooded highways and heavy traffic. So far it had worked out, and with the evacuations over, the number of cars on the highway in both directions was much lower.

As the caravan drove out of the school parking lot, the drivers noticed how much more intense the rain and wind had become just since they came. The light traffic helped, since their windshield wipers had trouble keeping up, and standing water on the road forced them to drive under twenty miles an hour.

When the convoy of graduates arrived at their dinner venue, they saw that the restaurant's outside neon sign was dark. A sign taped to the entrance read CLOSED FOR PRIVATE PARTY.

The owner ushered his guests through the dark dining room to a large banquet area in the back and asked for their attention. He told them that the storm had created some problems. Every employee but two — a cook and a server — had called in to advise they wouldn't be coming to work. The food delivery scheduled for today didn't happen because the truck didn't come from New Orleans. Because of all that, the items on tonight's menu were things on hand that required simple preparation. Chicken, fried shrimp or oysters, a half-dozen rib eyes, and a few filets of redfish were the only entree choices.

The restauranteur said the party must end at nine instead of midnight as they'd planned because he and his men had to get home. The attendees were thankful he had honored his commitment. Given the circumstances, no one would have blamed him for a last-minute cancellation.

Despite the food shortage, the owner had plenty of alcohol. He tended bar, serving rounds of drinks as the grads broke into small groups and swapped stories about the old days in Jeanerette.

Landry wondered about Craig. He'd missed the assembly and hadn't shown up here, but at last he arrived, ordered a gin and tonic, and joined the Cajun Cavalry. He seemed better; he would never be the life of a party, but he chatted and laughed with his friends, as he had done that first night.

"Remember the student council car wash?" Alain said. "Marty had a bunch of Smirnoff Ice in a cooler in his trunk. That little bitch Madeline Brewster couldn't wait to tell the principal on Monday morning. Remember what happened next?"

They laughed and laughed. "Yeah," Joe said. "We were two months from graduation and Marty had already been accepted to Tulane. The principal called him in and said he had one question for him. 'Marty,' he said, 'if you answer yes, I'm going to expel you.' Then he asked if you brought beer to the car wash."

Marty bellowed, "And I said to myself, 'It wasn't beer. It was Smirnoff Ice!' So I answered no, the principal avoided a major confrontation with my old man, and off to Tulane I went that fall!"

One story followed another, about Marty, or Joe, or Alain but never about Craig. He'd been the quiet one of the four, but tonight he seemed happy to be with them.

Landry had enough background for the human-interest story, but Landry sensed a much bigger story. He planned to corner Craig after dinner, because there might not be another opportunity. With the ceremony at St. Anne's postponed and how oddly Craig acted over the past twenty-four hours, Landry doubted he'd set foot in Iberia Parish again.

He didn't know what to make of Craig. Was he one of those people on the border between genius and insanity? Did memories trigger his trancelike states? And what secrets about the house and the cemetery was he harboring? Certain Craig wouldn't volunteer anything, he wondered how he'd find out more. He wanted to poke around the house on his own, but he didn't know how to do it. Today Craig had caught him in the house, but in his state, Landry doubted he knew he was there.

Coach Walker sat alone at a table, nursing a beer. Landry pulled up a chair and said, "I'm surprised you drove up here for this."

His old friend chuckled and said he and his wife spent every waking moment with each other. He said any chance for a few hours apart, even in a storm, seemed a blessing for both of them.

Coach was surprised to hear about Landry's visit to the cemetery and how Craig had seemed. "He's a smart enough guy," he said, "but he wasn't that great a student. I taught him world history. Actually, I should say he was in my class, because I can't say how much I taught him. He got a C, as I recall. He had the smarts, but he didn't care. He liked computers and math but not much else. That's why he went to St. Anne's instead of LSU or University of Louisiana Lafayette. His grades weren't good enough to get in the big schools, but it didn't matter to him. His parents made him go. They didn't care about anything else he did, but they insisted he go to college whether he wanted to or not. All of us teachers talked about the Morissets. They blamed us when he made less than straight As. They were the strangest people in Jeanerette, but nobody in town would cross them because they were rich and lived in a mansion."

At seven forty-five everyone ordered, and ten minutes later the lights flickered. It happened twice more, and the third time they stayed off. Gamely trying to give everyone a good experience, the owner brought in candles and announced they'd have dinner by candlelight. Since his stoves ran on gas, he promised the dinners would be out soon.

The rain beat down so hard on the building's tin roof that the classmates found it hard to talk. Landry checked the weather again. The wind velocity continued to weaken, but the storm stalled south of Morgan City, just sixty miles away, which increased the chance of heavy flooding here.

As they ate in the shadowy banquet room, Landry asked what else Coach remembered about Craig's family.

"His grandfather Albert lost his medical license. Biggest scandal that ever hit Jeanerette, according to my mother. He was a country doctor, like his father before him. Back in those days you didn't have to go to medical school. You could take the test and get a license based on experience. Guess you could lose it too."

"What happened?"

"People swept it under the rug, them being so rich and all. Before I tell you this, you gotta understand how people make up things about folks different from them. Some said the whole damned family, including Craig's mother and father, were doing weird experiments on animals and possibly humans too. I guess the medical licensing people got wind of it and nipped old Dr. Frankenstein in the bud."

Landry said, "I'll let you in on a secret. I was at the house today. The back door was unlocked and I looked around." He didn't mention the odd encounter with Craig. "You mentioned the real estate guy thinks the house will never sell because of those experiments and things. What else have you heard?"

Coach Walker took a draw from his beer and said, "You're not going to tell anyone these stories came from me, are you? This is a little town and I have to live here, you know."

Landry promised he wouldn't attribute a thing to him unless Coach allowed it.

"Those stories are the things my wife gets on to me about. They're rumors. It's a fact that the laboratory burned down. Everybody saw it. Far as I know, nobody's ever proved anything odd happened inside the house. But lots of folks sure have an opinion about it. They think all the Morissets were doing bizarre experiments."

He paused as the class president stood and clinked a glass with a spoon.

THE EXPERIMENTS: THE BAYOU HAUNTING 5

"Everyone, I hate to cut the festivities short, but I think we should all get where we're going for the night. Things are getting worse by the minute. I just got a call from the B&B where several of us are staying. The power's out and the parking lot is flooded. The owner told us to get back and hunker down. The rest of you live in the area or have rooms, I think. Is there anybody who doesn't have a place to stay tonight?"

Everybody was set, and shortly the tabs were brought out. The class president advised that Saturday's events — a tour of a plantation home and a final dinner at the country club in New Iberia — were cancelled. Classmates hugged each other, said their goodbyes, and sloshed through ankle-deep water to their cars.

Craig was out the door before Landry could catch him. When they got back to the hotel and if the bar was open, maybe he'd find him there. If not, there was always tomorrow morning. Landry and Coach were the last to leave. As the proprietor turned off the lights, he said, "Is there someplace we can go so you can tell me what you were going to say?"

Coach smiled. "You thinking there might be spooky stuff going on in your old hometown?"

"You got something spooky to tell me?"

"Tell you what," the older man said, taking Landry's arm and ushering him to the front door. "There's two places we can go to talk some more. One's the donut shop, but the other one would be way more interesting."

Landry was surprised at the man's enthusiasm. His face was positively beaming with excitement at the prospect of doing something daring. "Are you thinking what I'm thinking?"

Coach winked and said, "You said yourself the back door was unlocked. We can't be blamed for taking refuge from the storm."

"Okay, let's do it."

They took two cars, because Coach would go home from Amelia House, and Landry would return to the hotel in New Iberia. When they reached the Bayside drawbridge, they saw National Guard trucks lined up along the side of the road. Troops in ponchos huddled under trees, waiting for orders to close the bridge.

"If we go across, we may not be able to get back," Landry said.

"This isn't the only bridge. Another one might be open. My theory is, you only live once. What's Momma gonna do to me anyway, kill me?"

"Want to leave your car on this side, just in case?"

Coach Walker parked his pickup and rode with Landry. They crossed the bridge and turned onto the old highway. Down the road on the left Amelia House sat in the darkness, waiting for them.

CHAPTER TWELVE

Even more than the storm, Landry worried about Craig catching them in his house. Craig had left the restaurant early, and Landry presumed he and the others were back at the hotel by now.

When Landry left earlier, Craig had still been in the house, and he wondered if Craig had locked the door when he left. A part of him hoped so, because if they couldn't get in, this crazy visit would be over.

Another part of him — the part that always got him into trouble — cheered when the knob turned.

They didn't see Craig's Escalade, which Landry took as a good sign since he was about to break the law for the second time today. They walked inside and Landry asked Coach what he wanted to do.

"A picture's worth a thousand words. Let's look around and see what people gossip about — those experiments and all."

"Three doors upstairs are locked, and I should tell you something else. Craig caught me here this afternoon."

"Craig came in while you were nosing around? Wasn't that a little awkward?"

You don't know the half of it. "Finding me here didn't seem to bother him. That surprised me, but Craig's so strange that nothing he does should come as a surprise. He wasn't himself — that is, uh, I'm not sure what being himself really is, but he seemed detached and spaced out. Does that make sense?"

Coach nodded. "Did he show you around?"

"No. He seemed to be in a trance. I tried to talk to him and then I left. We were in an office at the other end of the house that's full of medical books, as you'd expect from a family of doctors."

Coach suggested they start at the top and work their way down. "Damned eerie place," he muttered as they climbed the darkened stairway with the light from Landry's phone. Tree branches buffeted by the wind cast spooky shadows through the windows. They danced and swayed back and forth on the walls in a ghostly waltz.

They had just reached the top floor when Landry's cell phone rang. Given the circumstances, the ringtone surprised the hell out of them. He didn't recognize the 239 area code or the number, but he thought it best to answer.

"Hello?"

It was Craig. "Where are you? Are you at the hotel?"

It's Craig, Landry mouthed, and Coach's eyes widened in alarm.

"I, uh, I stayed behind to talk to Coach Walker a little longer. I haven't seen him in years and we're just catching up. Why? What's up?"

"The owner asked if everyone had come back. He wants to lock up and go home. I didn't think you'd gotten back yet. I'll tell him to wait."

"No, that's not fair to him. Would you ask him to leave a key somewhere outside?"

"When will you be back?"

"It won't be long."

"Where are you?"

THE EXPERIMENTS: THE BAYOU HAUNTING 5

His questions made Landry uncomfortable because he stood in the upstairs hallway of Craig's house, lying through his teeth.

"Coach owns a café in town. We're just sitting here talking."

Craig said he'd text to let Landry know about the key and hung up.

Coach asked Landry if he thought they should leave.

"We've come this far, and Craig's in New Iberia. Let's finish what we came to do. Come on, we'll try the doors on this floor."

As Landry and Coach Walker walked to the first locked door and tried the knob, Craig Morisset parked next to Landry's Jeep. He sent a text telling Landry the key would be in a ziplock under the front door mat. Then he got out of his rental car, carefully closing the door even though in this storm no one would have heard anything.

Craig had been certain Landry would return. He recalled seeing Landry here earlier today, but in his state of paramnesia he couldn't recall anything specific. Tonight he felt normal again, and now anger filled his mind.

He left the dinner early and drove the Old Jeanerette Road to his house. He expected Landry would come, so he found a spot down the road to watch the house. He didn't have to wait long before the Jeep arrived.

It's just my house, *not my* home, he reminded himself as he crossed the porch and went inside. *But it's mine, and they had no right to enter without my permission.*

As he locked the door behind him, he heard them moving around somewhere upstairs. Nothing on the second floor would create a problem, but the third floor — that one was a different story. Those rooms had been the Morisset family quarters throughout the years. Most of them were bedrooms and parlors. But one was something else.

He paused at the second-floor landing and he could hear them talking. They were upstairs, where they had no right to be. They were in a place that could create grave danger for themselves. And for him.

Craig's mind was always spinning, and sometimes he thought odd or inappropriate things. Right now as he climbed the stairs, he thought of the child's game he and his brother had played.

No, not his brother. He didn't have a brother. He and a friend had played it. In the game, you got hotter as you came closer to whatever you were looking for.

Landry and Coach had been cold when he heard them talking earlier, but they were getting warmer with every step they took down the hallway. He peered through the railings and saw them halfway down the hall.

Hot! Hot! They're getting hot!

This was no game, and he had to stop things now. He reached the hall and walked toward them in the darkness.

Landry put his hand on the doorknob and tried it. Craig was certain it was locked, but the mere sight of someone touching it sent waves of fear and dread through his body.

"Stop it! Stop it right now!"

"Oh, shit," Coach said. "Hey, Craig. Now, listen. We can explain everything."

"Back away from that door!" he screamed.

Landry did what he demanded, stepping back and walking toward Craig. "I'm sorry —" he began, but he got cut off.

"I won't allow you to do this," Craig said, choking on his words as he spat them out. "Amelia House is mine. My family built it. This house isn't a place for cameramen to walk through, or for investigators like you to tell stories about, or for the public to watch the Morissets dragged through the mud like common people. They had their faults. Everyone does. But I won't let you expose them."

"What faults are you afraid I'll expose?" Landry asked. The moment the words came out, he wished he hadn't been confrontational.

THE EXPERIMENTS: THE BAYOU HAUNTING 5

"Get out! Get out of this house and leave us alone!"

The investigative reporter side of him appeared. Things moved fast and he had to take advantage of the moment. "Us? Who are you talking about, Craig? There's nobody left but you, and until today you hadn't set foot in his house since before your parents died. That's what you told me. That's what you tell everyone."

"What I've done is none of your business! Get out now or I'll call the police!"

Not in the middle of a hurricane when we're supposed to have evacuated, Landry thought, but now wasn't the time to argue a point.

"I told Coach about seeing your house today," he said. "I talked him into coming back here with me because he wanted to see it too. It's a showplace — a beautiful mansion filled with history and memories from over a hundred years ago. You've done a great job making sure it was maintained all these years. Your parents would be proud…"

Craig didn't respond, and a shadow over his face kept them from seeing his expression.

"Are you okay, buddy?" Coach said.

"This is no place for the living." The dead words in Craig's answer sounded even more sinister here in a darkened mansion during a frightful storm.

He walked past them to the door, withdrew a key from his pocket, inserted it and turned the lock. He walked inside and closed it behind him. They heard a solid click, then nothing.

"Might as well try the knob," Landry said. "We have nothing to lose."

Coach was flabbergasted. "Are you serious? What if…what if the door opens?"

"Then I guess we'll see what's behind it."

Muttering that he didn't really want to, Coach stood beside Landry as he tried to turn the knob. He breathed a sigh of relief when it wouldn't open.

They had to obey Craig's command and face the music in the morning. Coach was off the hook — there would be no more reunion parties this weekend, so he wouldn't have to face Craig in the light of day. But Landry would, and he wondered how he'd explain being inside the house not once without permission, but twice in the same day.

CHAPTER THIRTEEN

Saturday Morning

Landry arrived back at the hotel with no way to get inside, since there was no key under the mat. But he was in luck. It wasn't late and someone was still downstairs — one of the reunion guys had fixed himself a nightcap and was plodding through the lobby when Landry knocked.

Throughout the night rain hammered hard against the windows, and Landry awoke several times. Once he heard people talking in the hallway. Later he heard a car engine and thought more evacuees might have arrived. He lay awake that time, knowing that in a few hours he had to vacate his room and perhaps become a refugee himself.

He awoke at ten past seven as half-light filtered through the window. The low clouds seemed more ominous than yesterday, and sporadic gusts of wind played with the rain. He looked down into the parking lot. An electric car sat in water that reached the bottom of its doors, the unfortunate owner having parked his small vehicle in the wrong spot, and the Escalade was gone.

Despite no electricity, several people were in the breakfast room. An LED camping lantern sat on each table, and the light made the room seem cozy. Scrambled eggs and crisp bacon cooked on a gas range sat on a buffet along with milk and juice. The only essential Landry didn't see was coffee, and he hoped he'd find some of that soon.

A family he hadn't seen yesterday — a man and his wife with two small children — sat at a table. Two alumni were at another, their rolling bags parked against the wall behind them. The three Cavalrymen — Marty, Alain and Joe — sipped Bloody Marys with their breakfasts.

A battery-operated radio was tuned to New Iberia's radio station KANE. There was only weather, because that was all that mattered to anyone whose radio could pick up the signal.

Overnight the slow-moving storm had turned more to the north. Still dumping rain, it sat west of Napoleonville, about fifty miles east of New Iberia. The weatherman said it would rain all day — they'd get six to eight more inches — and said most highways in Iberia and Lafayette Parishes had been closed because of high water. For listeners who'd decided to stay, he cautioned there might be long-term power outages.

Landry joined the two alumni at their table. "I see your bags," he said. "Do you have far to go?"

"No, thank God. My parents live in Lafayette and his in Broussard. They have power and we're going there a night or two until things blow over. The Cavalry are the ones I worry about. Marty and Craig flew here, and Alain and Joe drove, but the roads are all closed. Where will you go?"

Landry said he wasn't sure and asked about the family across the room. The guys said when they returned last night, they were in the lobby, exhausted from a fifty-mile, three-hour drive. They had left their home in Wyandotte and made it this far before giving up for the night. They hoped to spend the night in the lobby.

THE EXPERIMENTS: THE BAYOU HAUNTING

"When we came in, the owner asked us if we minded moving in together so those folks could have a room. He was prepared to let them sleep in the lobby, but he said with little kids, they needed a good night's sleep. I gave up my room, so they had a bed for the night."

He asked about Craig, but they hadn't seen him since dinner. Then he walked to Marty's table and asked what they planned to do.

"We might go fishing," Marty replied. "Pretty soon the parking lot will be deep enough to catch a big one."

Alain said, "Better watch out for alligators," and Landry said that wasn't a joking matter. He asked about Craig, but no one knew anything. With his usual lack of tact, Marty said, "He's turned strange since he made all that money after high school. Notice how he zones out when he's in the middle of a conversation? It's damned hard to talk to him when he's in zombie mode."

Alain was kinder. "It's like being around people makes him uptight. He's so awkward, other people feel it too."

Joe shushed them and cocked his head toward the lobby as Craig walked into the breakfast room, pulled over a chair from another table, and sat down with them. His windbreaker and jeans were soaked, and he had something the others coveted — a travel mug of coffee.

"Morning," Landry said. After last night, he couldn't imagine what Craig's reaction would be, but Craig gave a wave and said hello.

Marty wasted no time on pleasantries. "I didn't see your car in the lot this morning. Where were you, and where the hell did you get coffee?"

"I couldn't sleep, so I got up early and drove down to Jeanerette to see if my house was okay. I was also seeing if the highway was open, and it is. There's a lot of flooding but almost no traffic. I stayed on 182 all the way into town and made it just fine, but I'm also driving a heavy SUV, and that helped. Jeanerette's full of National Guard. One of them told me the highway south of town was closed. The Teche has flooded in a lot of areas, but the Bayside bridge is still open. You'd be amazed how high the water is. It's up to the bottom of the bridge itself, and it's in my yard, but not in the house.

"Oh, and how about this coffee! You want to know where I got it? I told you I hadn't been back to the house since 2003, and how I'd left instructions not to get rid of things. Well, the power was on, a sealed can of Maxwell House was in the pantry, and the can opener was in the same drawer as always. I made myself a pot of coffee. But enough of that — there's something important we need to talk about."

As he listened to Craig's answer, Landry thought he sounded more *normal*, if that was the right word, than any time previously. He knew part of his story was a lie and wondered if he'd come back last night or stayed at Amelia House until just a few minutes ago.

Landry was surprised at how outgoing Craig seemed. Maybe it was because he had something people wanted to hear besides answering questions about his success. He seemed to have a sense of purpose, and in a moment, Landry understood what that purpose was.

Craig told them they must find a place to spend the night. The storm wouldn't abate for at least twenty-four hours, which meant the rivers and bayous would continue to rise, which meant more highways would close, and at some point so would all the bridges in Iberia Parish. If you were on one side of Bayou Teche, there would be no crossing to the other.

"We're all in the same boat. Alain, you live in Lake Charles, but the roads are closed, so you can't get back. Joe and Landry have to drive to New Orleans, but they can't get there either. And you, Marty — you have to go to the Lafayette airport. A soldier told me you can still get to Lafayette, but the airport's closed at least until Monday.

THE EXPERIMENTS: THE BAYOU HAUNTING 5

My pilot's picking me up at the airport in New Iberia, but he can't fly in until who knows when.

"We have to check out of here by nine, and we'll go to my house in Jeanerette. It's secure and has all the comforts of home, 2003 style, and we can weather the storm. We should go soon before they shut down the Bayside drawbridge and we can't get to the house."

Astonished at his offer, Landry sat quietly, waiting to hear from the others.

Marty said, "Until Thursday, you hadn't been back here since your parents died. Do you believe it's a good idea to spend the night in the house? To tell the truth, I'm concerned about your mental condition. Sometimes you seem to zone out on us a little. Facing your past might not be the best thing for you to do today, especially with other people around."

Landry had bigger concerns than that. Except for Craig, the men at the table had no idea he had been in the house twice in the past twenty-four hours, and so had Craig. Marty called Craig's trances "zoning out on us a little," but that didn't do it justice. What if he did something dangerous while he "zoned out"? No one could predict if or when, but it could happen.

Craig brushed aside Marty's comment, and Landry heard another lie. "Until an hour ago I hadn't seen my house since 2003. I have a property management company that takes care of it, but nobody's spent a night in it ever since. I looked around this morning and fixed some coffee, and everything went fine. There are a lot of memories in there, but every old house has memories. Who better to face them with than my buddies from the Cajun Cavalry? It's Amelia House or spend the night in your car. Which do you choose?"

All this time, he had never appeared upset or angry at Landry. It was as if he didn't remember — or chose to ignore — his encounter with Landry and Coach Walker.

"Am I invited too?" Landry asked. "I'm not an insider like you guys."

"With one stipulation, of course you are," Craig said. "While you're a guest in my family home, everything that happens is completely off the record."

Landry shook his head. "I'd really like to join you all, and not just because I don't relish spending the night in my Jeep. But as a journalist I have to explain something. My personal experiences and observations are always on the record. If you allow me to join you, that's part of the deal. You four are old friends and I respect that. I don't intend to publicize anything personal about your friendship unless you allow me to. But the experience of an owner staying in his childhood home for the first time in seventeen years is something noteworthy. I want to come with you. I want to see a house that's frozen back in 2003, but my personal experiences at Amelia House are on the record."

Craig hesitated, and Marty said, "Hell, Craig, what do you think's gonna happen in there? Do you have ghosts in the woodwork? What the hell is he gonna see?"

This time Marty went too far. "Cut him a little slack," Landry shot back. "His parents died on the grounds. There are a lot of memories, like he said."

Craig jerked his head up. "How do you know where my parents died?"

"I read a news article about it." It wasn't how Landry knew, but it was the truth. Being such a small town, everyone in Jeanerette knew everything. Landry had been twelve when the Morissets died, and he didn't recall the event, but he would have heard about it at the time. Two prominent, wealthy citizens perishing together on their property would have been all that people talked about.

After the morbid discussion about his family, it surprised Landry that Craig's demeanor continued to be upbeat, given his penchant for "zoning out."

THE EXPERIMENTS: THE BAYOU HAUNTING 5

He replied to Landry, "It's not fair not to allow you to come when you have no place to go. Just remember to be fair in return if anything unusual happens at Amelia House. So what'll it be, men? My place or your cars for the night?"

"You believe something's gonna happen, and I want to know what it is," Marty grumbled, but Craig stood, declared he had to pack, and left the room. Landry wanted to catch him alone and ask him about last night, but the opportunity never arose, and he wondered if Craig would remember.

They checked out and Craig led the convoy to Jeanerette. It took almost thirty minutes and when they got to Bayside Street, they turned left to take the drawbridge, but now an army truck blocked the road. A sergeant approached Craig's car and said the Teche was lapping over the bridge and still rising. He wouldn't allow them to cross.

"How about the Lewis Street bridge?" Craig asked, referring to the next bridge south. The sergeant shook his head. "Every bridge in the parish south of here is closed too."

Craig explained that they had nowhere else to go, and his family home sat less than a half-mile away on the other side. He said he had four friends with him, casually dropping Landry's name and his own.

The man knew exactly who they were, and his demeanor reflected it. "You're Craig Morisset? It's nice to meet you! And Landry Drake's with you too? Wait 'til my wife hears about this! She's a big fan. Which vehicle is he in?"

Craig answered and asked if he would let them pass. He agreed but said that they couldn't return until the water receded. It could be hours or days. Craig said it wasn't a problem; if necessary, they would use the old highway to get back to New Iberia.

The procession crept across the creaky drawbridge as water from the raging river sloshed over it. Craig had never seen it this high. In his rearview mirror he watched the sergeant talking to Landry, and he was thankful the name-dropping had worked. He almost never did it, much preferring privacy to ostentation, but today it was useful.

Everyone parked and Craig ran to the porch, motioning for the others to join him. Landry saw him take a key from his pocket and realized that somewhere in the past twenty-four hours he must have found one.

They stripped down to their underwear just inside the back door and threw their soggy clothes and shoes in a bin Craig brought from the laundry room. His parents had installed modern appliances, and as long as the power stayed on, the clothes dryer would serve them well.

As if looking around, Landry strolled to the other end of the house and found the office door closed and locked.

"Everyone go to the second floor and pick out a bedroom," Craig told his friends. "There are five up there, all ready to go. I'll sleep —"

He paused. He was about to say he'd use his old bedroom on the third floor, but something stopped him.

"You guys pick first. There's plenty of room."

While the others carried their luggage upstairs and changed into dry clothes, Craig put on a sweatshirt and pants in the kitchen. He opened the pantry, wondering if there was anything fit to eat. Even if a store somewhere might be open, they couldn't cross the bridge now. This morning when he'd found the coffee, he'd seen shelves filled with canned goods, but now he took a closer look.

The men looking after the house had followed his instructions well. Everything remained as it had been the day his parents died. Although perishables like bread and eggs had been discarded long ago, he found long-expired cans of vegetables and fruit, sleeves of pasta, two more large tins of coffee, and a dozen of those little cans of

THE EXPERIMENTS: THE BAYOU HAUNTING 5

Vienna sausages. Those brought back a rare fond memory about his parents and made him smile. His father had loved them, although he and his mother detested the stuff.

How odd that I recall what my father liked to eat, he thought. *I can't remember my parents ever spending time with me, but I remember Vienna sausages.*

He looked in the refrigerator and was surprised to find two six-packs of Dixie beer he assumed some workman would have appropriated ages ago. Someone called his name, and he yelled, "In the kitchen!" Marty came in, and Craig showed him the cans of food. "You're the doctor, so you tell me. Is it okay to eat this stuff?"

"Sure. As long as the cans aren't punctured or dented or bloated, the contents should be fine. Maybe it won't taste as good as in 2003, but it's edible. You like Vienna sausages?"

"I'd rather starve, thanks."

"Mind if I check them out?"

"It's your funeral," Craig said, only half-joking. Marty used the tab to peel back the lid and showed Craig the little meat sticks standing like soldiers. He drained the can, shook the sausages out on a napkin and stuck one in his mouth.

"Tastes just like always," he proclaimed, and Craig said if that's how they tasted, he'd pass.

He handed Marty cans of baked beans, new potatoes, green beans, turnip greens and chili. The doctor looked them over, tossed a couple, and put the rest on the counter. As the others filtered in, he explained how canned food lasts indefinitely. Unconvinced, they watched him eat another seventeen-year-old sausage, and Joe said he believed he'd wait a while before eating, to see if Marty died.

At 10:43 a.m. the power failed.

CHAPTER FOURTEEN

The clothes dryer stopped mid-cycle as the house was plunged into gloom punctuated by a weak half-light from outside. The storm showed no signs of weakening, and the men started assessing what resources they had if the power stayed off.

Everyone had portable cell phone chargers, and two had car plug-ins. Since the stove in the kitchen ran on natural gas, they would have hot food, and everyone but Landry and Craig had brought beer and alcohol in coolers. They seemed in good shape to wait out twenty-four hours of bad weather. They considered themselves fortunate to have a dry place to stay, a fully stocked house, and plenty to eat and drink.

Craig had played with his father's poker chips as a child, and he found them and a deck of cards in a huge old cabinet in the parlor. He took two boxes of candles from the pantry, kept by his mother for an occasion just like this, and soon the dining room table became the focus of a low-stakes poker game illuminated by the candles in two beautiful candelabras. Alain commented that it was like being in the Addams family mansion.

Around noon the lights came on. Since Marty hadn't died from food poisoning, the rest decided they'd eat the food. They warmed up chili, pork and beans and weenies and ate at the kitchen table, beers in hand. Someone commented that life was good.

After lunch, everyone retired to their bedrooms for an afternoon nap. They were doing it more to pass the time than anything else, and some of them read on iPads and phones while others dozed off. The power flickered twice but otherwise remained on.

At 3:41 p.m. the back door flew open and crashed into the wall with a resounding thud. Craig came down from the top floor and met the others to see what had happened.

Rain cascaded in through the open door. Craig pushed it shut against the wind and glanced outside, surprised at how high the river had risen in the few hours since they arrived. A few feet from the porch now, it was much higher than he'd ever seen it.

Craig said, "I don't know how the door could have blown open."

"That's crazy," Marty said. "I watched you lock it earlier."

"I guess I didn't secure it," Craig said, knowing he had.

Alain asked about Joe, and the rest of them noticed for the first time he wasn't there.

Marty snorted. "Passed out, maybe. He had a flask in his back pocket when he went upstairs for his 'nap.' He couldn't hear a cannon go off by now."

"Let him sleep," Alain said. "I don't blame him for drinking. There's nothing else to do, and I think I'll have a little nip myself."

By five they had gathered in the living room. No one spoke; all their stories and catching up had happened over the past two nights. These guys who had been inseparable twenty years ago had nothing in common now but the past, and they had spent hours covering the old days. Joe still hadn't come downstairs, and Marty said he'd roust him out if he hadn't shown up by dinnertime.

The lights went out again around six, and Craig moved the candelabras into the cavernous room Craig said his grandfather had named the Great Room. Although it was warm and humid outdoors, the gloom inside the house made things cool and drafty. Wood lay in a rack next to the big rock fireplace, but it was so old and dry it would only work for kindling. But they had an alternative. Recently someone had taken down a diseased tree and stacked a rick of cut wood on the back porch. It was wet, but eventually it would catch. Marty and Alain brought in several logs, used the dry wood as starter, and soon the sticks popped and smoked. It took some effort to keep it going, but soon they had a roaring fire that cast eerie shadows about the room.

They opened Marty's liter of vodka. Marty and Landry fixed themselves martinis while the others cut theirs with some tonic water Alain had brought. Sitting in leather armchairs around the fire, the conversation turned to the house and its occupants over the decades.

Craig told them each floor had twenty-three hundred square feet. This room, the Great Room, measured sixty by forty feet and had fourteen-foot ceilings. It was by far the largest room in the house, and portraits occupied the spaces between beautiful dark wood cabinets and bookshelves. Stone-faced ancestors glared down at them as if irritated by the noisy intrusion after years of solitude.

"Who are these people?" Landry asked, and Craig listed them one by one. Landry recalled the names — he'd taken pictures of their crypts at the cemetery yesterday. But they came alive as he saw their faces. The formal demeanor, hawklike nose and high starched collar of Marco, the Frenchman who built the house. The frown of his wife, Amelia. His son, Albert — Craig's grandfather — who stood in front of this very fireplace, wearing a white doctor's coat, and had an old-fashioned stethoscope draped around his neck. Here was a man who wanted the world to remember that he was a doctor, even though he'd lost the license that gave him that title.

The next picture was of Albert's wife Genevieve. She stood in the wide center hallway, wearing a long white gown and the only smile of the entire lot. Behind her the house was gaily decorated for Mardi Gras, and she held a purple, green and gold carnival mask.

"It's the only one that's a photograph," Craig commented. "It's from 1975. There are no other pictures showing the house decorated. Maybe they were throwing a party — nobody knows for sure but look at her smile. All the rest look like they're going to a funeral." *He's right*, Landry mused. Their countenances ranged from peeved to angry.

The last — a portrait of Craig's parents — was of more recent vintage. In nineteen-seventies clothing and sporting trendy hairstyles, Frank and Maria were in one painting. She sat on the piano bench across the room and he stood next to her with his elbow resting on the instrument. They too were stern-faced and impassive. No smiles for these two; Landry wondered if they were that way in life.

Marty said he remembered Craig's father from the old days, but couldn't recall what line of work he'd been in.

"He didn't work in the traditional sense. For one thing, he played the stock market. When they opened a brokerage office in town, he'd spend hours there researching stocks and making trades."

"But your grandfather and great-grandfather were doctors, right?"

"You have a good memory."

Marty took another sip of his martini and furrowed his brow. "Wasn't there something about your grandfather…something about being a doctor that got him in trouble?"

THE EXPERIMENTS: THE BAYOU HAUNTING 5

Landry watched a veil pass over Craig's face. He was withdrawing.

Fueled by the alcohol, Marty didn't notice and pushed harder. "Didn't he lose his medical license? I think I remember something —"

Craig stood, looked around the room as if no one else was there, and walked to the fireplace, where he stared at the dancing flames. Although still here, he had left his friends again, going back into a place deep inside his mind. Landry wondered if this was something he'd dealt with his entire life, and if it was a mental condition or something else.

Alain stood and said, "We need to check on Joe. He's been upstairs for almost four hours." He, Landry and Marty went upstairs, leaving Craig by himself.

Marty rapped on Joe's bedroom door and shouted, "Hey, asshole! You're missing all the fun!"

Hearing nothing, he tried the knob, but the door was locked.

"Joe! Joe, wake up! It's six thirty!"

Nothing.

Marty said, "Landry, run down and get Craig. I'll keep trying the door."

"Alain, will you go?" Landry said. "This is what I do for a living. Something's going on, and I need to find out what it is."

While Alain went downstairs, Landry and Marty went into the bedrooms on either side, looking for a door that adjoined Joe's.

"Wait!" Landry shouted. "The porch! There's a door on that side. Maybe it's unlocked."

The bedrooms opened onto a long, shared veranda overlooking the bayou. They went into Marty's room and unlocked the French double doors. The gale-force winds made it difficult to push the doors open, and rain poured into the room. Marty stepped out first.

"Damn, it's slick out here. Watch your step!" He pressed his body against the house and inched toward a matching set of French doors twelve feet away. Landry followed, and the amazing power of the storm took him by surprise. Winds that seemed to blow from every direction buffeted them, and they were drenched within seconds.

"I see him!" Marty screamed into the wind as Landry reached the door, tried the knob, and found it locked. They could see Joe lying on the bed across the room. Landry banged on the door, and Marty shouted his name, but he didn't stir.

Landry yelled, "I think he's passed out. It's crazy out here! Let's go back inside and try to get in his room from there! At least we won't be blown off the porch!"

As they made their way back, Landry looked through the mist toward the bayou. A hundred yards away something out there moved slowly across the yard toward the tree line. He thought maybe it was a person dressed in dark clothing, slogging through ankle-deep water toward the woods. The visibility was terrible, especially with night fast approaching, and it could easily also have just been a stray cow.

"Marty, look! Do you see something out there?" He pointed, but there was nothing now. Marty pushed him along, and they ducked back inside to find Alain waiting for them. From the look on his face, they knew something was very wrong.

"I can't find Craig. He's not in the Great Room. I looked around everywhere on the first floor, but I can't find him."

"What do you mean you can't find him?" Marty said as he emerged from the bathroom with two towels, one of which he tossed to Landry. "We left him in front of the fireplace five minutes ago."

"Yeah, and he was in that trance. He's gone, I'm telling you."

"Dammit, man. That's crazy talk. He has to be somewhere. Get back down there and find him. I've got to get into Joe's room."

Landry wondered if the hazy figure he'd seen moving across the yard was Craig. He was wearing a dark shirt, and minutes after they left him alone, Landry had seen what could have been a person slogging toward the woods.

"I may know where he is. Come on! He may be in trouble!"

Marty cried, "What about Joe?"

Landry said, "Alain, come with me. Craig may be outside. I think I saw him. Marty, you're a doctor. Stay here, figure out how to get inside, and make sure Joe's okay."

Their windbreakers were no match for the storm's fury. They stepped into the water and waded out into the expansive front yard as if they were fording a stream. Every step was an effort, but at last they came to a place near where Landry had seen the figure.

"Craig! Craig, can you hear me?"

The wind howled, making it difficult to hear anything. As they went into the woods, the ground level rose, which meant less water to slog through, and the canopy of tall oaks deflected some of the rain. Landry yelled for him again, and they heard something.

"I'm here."

He stood in a clearing fifty feet from them and appeared not to know who they were.

"Craig, it's me, Landry! We were in the house, but you walked away. Do you remember?"

He stared at Alain and Landry and then looked down at something in his hand.

Landry saw he was holding a key.

"What was this place?" Alain asked. Craig pointed to a concrete block foundation that lay before them.

Landry knew what it had been. It was the building Coach mentioned, the outbuilding where the fire happened.

"Your parents died here, didn't they? This was the laboratory."

Craig stared at the foundation and held up the key. "Here's how you get inside. I took it," he said in robotic words. "I stole a key ring from my father's dresser drawer. If they couldn't get in here, they'd have to pay attention to me. What crazy things a child thinks. By keeping them away from the one thing they cared about, they would care about me instead.

"My father had another key, so my plan didn't work. They didn't have to pay attention after all. My father never figured out that I took his key. This afternoon I remembered it, and there it was, right where I hid it when I was eleven years old."

Alain said, "What the hell's he talking about?"

Landry put a finger to his lips. "Are you saying they spent a lot of time here?"

"They had a room in the house they also called a laboratory, but neither were laboratories. The one in the house was for experiments, but Mother and Father spent more time here, where all the records were, dating back to Great-grandfather Marco. This was where they did their research."

"The servants became my de facto parents. They sat with me at meals, taught me how to fish and hunt, bought my clothes, took me to school — everything. I loved them and they loved me."

He gazed at the foundation. His remembrances came out as pitiful, mournful words. "A long time ago, long before I stole the key, I came here one day and opened the door. They were inside. He beat me and threatened to do worse if I ever came spying on them again.

"Spying. That's what he called it. I was a kid and I thought if I knew what they were doing, maybe they'd let

THE EXPERIMENTS: THE BAYOU HAUNTING 5

me help, or tell me about it. I told myself I'd act interested no matter what. I'd pretend it was the most important thing to me, like it was to my parents. But my father never let me go inside."

"You never went in there during your entire childhood? Your parents were still alive when you went to college, right? They ignored you for eighteen years, and you never saw what they were doing?"

Craig turned to face Landry, his countenance eerie and spectral. He looked like a ghoul with his stringy wet hair, dead eyes and blank stare.

"That's not what I said. I found out everything. What they did in the house and what they did in this building. I knew all of it."

CHAPTER FIFTEEN

Saturday Evening

With Alain holding Craig by one arm and Landry the other, they guided him back through the rainstorm. He seemed to perk up by the time they reached the house and stripped down for the second time in a few hours.

"We have to stop going outdoors because I'm running out of clothes," Alain said, and Landry agreed. With the power off, the other ones were drying in front of the fire, so they hung these on a rack in the laundry room.

As they climbed the stairs, Landry called out to Marty, who shouted for them to come to Joe's bedroom. He was sitting on the side of the bed next to his friend, who lay on his back with a washcloth over his eyes.

"Everything okay?" Landry asked as Marty laughed at the three men standing in the doorway in their underwear.

"Bizarre, but okay. Get some clothes on and I'll explain everything."

In moments they were back. Marty asked them to gather close around the bed. He explained that he'd broken a pane in the French door on the porch to gain entry to the room, and he'd found Joe unconscious in the bed. There was an empty pint of vodka on the nightstand and a glass with some almost-melted ice cubes in the bottom.

"Is he okay?" Alain asked. Joe raised his head a little and nodded.

Marty explained what had happened when he tried to wake Joe. "I think he fell and hit something. Once I got him awake, I examined his eye. He says there's no pain, but he can't explain it. Neither can I. I've never seen anything like this before."

Joe reached an unsteady hand to the washcloth and pulled it away. The skin around his left eye socket was beginning to turn purple. He opened his eyes, and the men gasped at his blood-red eyeball.

"Some kind of trauma for sure," Marty said. "I wonder if he had a bit too much vodka and fell on something, hitting himself in the eye. He doesn't remember anything."

"I had a couple of drinks and took a nap," Joe murmured. "I had one hell of a bad dream, but I can't remember what it was, and then Marty woke me up. I have a throbbing in the left side of my head from whatever happened, but I'll be fine."

Rain was coming through the broken windowpane, and Landry asked Craig if there was some wood they could tack over the hole, but he had left the room. He walked into the hall and called his name. Craig didn't answer, but if he'd gone downstairs, he wouldn't have heard.

Joe said he felt good enough to go down, but he was so unsteady they walked him to the Great Room. It was almost dark, and they found Craig rebuilding the fire. He helped Landry scrounge up materials to fix the windowpane and brought out the remaining candles. Marty told Joe to stretch out on the couch, and he used ice cubes from the freezer to fashion an ice pack for his eye. He appeared disoriented and slurred his words. Marty asked him questions, but he

THE EXPERIMENTS: THE BAYOU HAUNTING 5

couldn't remember the simplest things like his last name or where he was.

Marty figured he had suffered a mild concussion. "Taking a fall and hitting something would be consistent with the bruising around his eye and his temporary loss of memory."

Craig heated up more canned food — pork and beans this time — and they ate in silence in front of the fire. He provided a treat along with their beanie weenies — a twenty-five-year-old bottle of Cabernet Sauvignon from his father's wine cellar. Everyone but Joe, who sat staring at his food, had a glass.

Suddenly the room burst into light. Their eyes having been accustomed to a gloomy half-light from the candles, they squinted and shouted a "hooray." Marty looked at the weather app on his phone and gave them another bit of good news. The storm was moving away from them. It would pass west of Baton Rouge around daybreak. They walked onto the porch and saw that the rain and the western sky seemed lighter. It would be hours before the standing water receded, but things were looking up.

The positive turn of events seemed to buoy Craig's spirits, and he became conversant and animated once again. Joe wasn't so lucky; he complained of a dull headache. He didn't participate in the discussions. He just lay on the couch with the ice pack on his eye.

"Didn't this house have an elevator?" Marty asked. "Didn't we get drunk and ride it up and down one night when your parents left town? Remember that, Joe?"

Joe said nothing. He didn't seem to realize that Marty had spoken to him.

Craig said Marty was remembering the dumbwaiter his father later sealed up. "They didn't need it. In fact, we never knew why my great-grandfather had it installed. My mother thought it could be to haul water upstairs for the wash bowls and chamber pots. Except for our midnight ride, I can't recall anybody ever using it."

As the words came out, a chill swept over him. He shuddered, hoped the others hadn't seen, and turned his face away so they couldn't see the fear — the remembering.

Jerry. A long time ago, Jerry had showed him the dumbwaiter and forced him to ride in it.

He heard a voice, a distant sound. Someone was talking to him.

Craig, is the dumbwaiter in your father's office?

Landry had spoken. He saw Landry sitting on the sofa next to him, but his voice echoed in a misty fog that blotted out Craig's thoughts. He was in another place but also in *this* place, the house where bad things happened a long time ago.

Did he ride the dumbwaiter again? Yesterday? Or today? Did he, did he dream it, something like what his brain was doing to him right now — a twisted, flowing mixture of reality and memory and flashbacks to this room when his parents lived here. And to that other room. The other one…

He struggled to finish that memory, and at last it came to him — fuzzy, in bits and pieces, but enough. Yes, he rode the dumbwaiter today. He went upstairs in the dumbwaiter when everyone went to their bedrooms, and he — what? What was it?

Then he remembered.

Oh my God! What have I done?

CHAPTER SIXTEEN

Craig shook his head as if that might loosen the cobwebs and clarify the vague recollections. Even as he did so, different thoughts flashed through his mind. Other memories. Hidden things. Family secrets that one must never talk about.

Hold this over his nose. Careful! You're pushing too hard. Let him breathe it in.

Hand me the orbitoclast. No, you idiot! Not that one — the one to the left! Just forget it. Maria, hand me the tool. He's never going to be of any help.

I never asked to help you, Father. I didn't want to learn your work, but you forced me, because you thought I would embrace it like you and Mother did.

The day they died was the greatest day of my life. I vowed I would never return.

What in God's name made me agree to come back? Now I can never leave. The things I managed to forget have crowded back into my brain. Because of those memories, I have become just like him. *I know too much.*

Craig's biggest fear about returning had been that the lapses would start again, and he'd been right.

BILL THOMPSON

Once he left for college and got away from his parents, he'd been a different person — free and in control of every situation. He took an idea and built a company that he sold for an unbelievable sum. The fire brought an end to Frank and Maria Morisset, and he arranged no funeral because their deaths brought only relief, not the sadness that permeated every fiber of his being while he lived with them. The medical examiner handed over their charred bodies and sent him a bill for hauling them to the morgue. He paid it with a sigh of relief that this chapter was finished.

The memory lapses stopped in 2003. Seventeen years without the torment. But the moment he returned to Iberia Parish, so did they. He had experienced some since he arrived on Thursday, but he didn't know how many, because sometimes he wasn't aware when they happened. The problem was that others had seen him. Being around other people was always a problem, but he was at his most vulnerable in this house, and four other people were watching his every move. Especially Landry Drake, the worst possible person to have around. He couldn't allow Landry to learn the truth. But how could he avoid it when he was having lapses?

Damn the hurricane. I should have been back in Key Largo by now, but I'm trapped in my parents' house.

I can't let the memories take over my mind. Things will get worse and worse until I can't come back.

They're already getting worse. Look at my poor friend Joe.

CHAPTER SEVENTEEN

Saturday Night

"Craig?" Landry repeated, realizing that he'd slipped into another fugue. "Is the dumbwaiter in your father's office?"

Craig snapped out of the lapse. He had no recollection of his encounter with Landry yesterday at the house and wondered how Landry could have known where it was.

Be careful. You may have said something earlier that you don't remember.

"Yes, which is why I think it wasn't for hauling water. If that were so, wouldn't it have started in the kitchen? Truth is, no one knows why my ancestor included an elevator. I think it was just a novelty — something to show off that the neighbors didn't have."

For a spur-of-the-moment response, he hoped the answer was believable enough to satisfy them.

Then Landry asked if they could see it.

Shit. "Why would you want to?" he stammered. "No. No, I don't think we can. My father boarded it up a long time ago."

"Can you at least show me where it was? Your house is fascinating, and a secret elevator makes it even more special." What Landry actually wanted was to learn if it was in the corner where Craig had disappeared.

Marty switched subjects before Craig could answer. He bellowed, "How about a tour of the third floor? We only have one night, and I want to see more of the house. How about those locked doors upstairs? Is that where your old man kept the skeletons in the closet?" He and Alain laughed, but Landry watched Craig's facial expression and saw the difficult time he was having.

Alain said, "Craig, when Landry and I found you in the woods, you mentioned a laboratory in the house where your parents did experiments. Is that one of the locked rooms? That might be an interesting one to see, if you're up to it."

The pressure on Craig mounted with every request, and Landry feared he'd slip out of reality again.

"Guys, let's respect Craig's feelings. He hasn't been in this house in years, and he's doing a hell of a lot better than I would be in the same situation. We need to allow the man a little time to reflect on the past without putting pressure on him."

Craig was determined to get through this without breaking down. He would show them enough to satisfy them while keeping the secrets.

"I appreciate the thought, Landry, but it's okay. You all are right — there are lots of ghosts in this house. You might call them skeletons in the closet, but to me they're memories of things that happened years ago. The dumbwaiter isn't boarded up — I just preferred not to show it to you. Come with me. I'll show you where it is." They walked to the office, leaving Joe on the couch.

As Landry expected, he walked to the corner where he'd disappeared yesterday. Landry had examined the panels, the adjoining bookshelf and floorboards, but he didn't know how he vanished. Now Craig stood in the corner and moved his hand to the second shelf on his left. He pushed the first book inwards, revealing a tiny button that he pressed before sliding the book back to its original place.

A panel slid silently into the wall behind the bookcase, revealing a three-foot opening five feet high. Craig stepped inside and said, "Come get me if this thing doesn't work. No one's used it in a long time." He closed the panel and Landry recognized the sound — the faint creaking and grinding of gears.

Craig himself had used the dumbwaiter, and Landry knew it. Why did he need to lie about it?

"I'll be damned!" Marty said. "I remember it now!" He pushed in the book and pressed the button. The panel slid open to reveal a tight space where the dumbwaiter had been. He stuck his head inside and looked up. "There it is. He took it up one floor."

"Are you looking for something?" They turned and found Craig standing behind them, smiling at their surprise.

"How the hell did you get here?" Alain asked.

"The easy way. I took the stairs."

"How do you bring the dumbwaiter back?" Landry asked, and Craig showed him an up-down button on the wall inside the shaft. He pressed it, closed the panel, and the car returned.

"Where does it go?"

"To bedrooms on the second and third floors."

"Can I have a ride?" Alain asked, and Marty said he wanted to go next.

Craig spoke firmly. "No, and I shouldn't have used it myself. It isn't safe. The maintenance people don't know it's here, so there's been no upkeep in years. I promised to let you see it, and I did." He closed the panel and offered to take them to the third floor.

As they walked upstairs, he told them some rooms were off-limits. "I'm not going into my parents' private quarters.

I'm a grown man, but there are some demons that I choose not to confront. I hope you understand. Regardless, you aren't going inside."

He opened one of the unlocked doors on the bayou side of the house. "As a child, this was my room," he said. Alain and Marty remembered it. They weren't here much, and then only when Craig's parents went out of town for some meeting or seminar.

They saw twin beds, an overstuffed chair and matching ottoman, a dresser and a desk with a chair. But the one thing that caught everyone's eyes were the books. Shelves ran along the wall that faced the bayou. Stuffed with texts, they extended to the ceiling and were separated by the same tall French doors as in the other bedrooms, the ones that opened out onto the second-floor porch. There was no organization to the volumes on shelves; large books and small, paperbacks, old leather-bound tomes and textbooks sat next to each other in a haphazard, jumbled mess with not a single empty space.

"My God," Landry said. "Look at the books! All yours?"

"Yes. With two super-intelligent parents insisting I read, I learned to love books. You might say I was an avid reader."

You might also say that books allowed me to escape from reality.

Landry looked at a few titles. They covered an incredibly wide range of subjects, and many were worn and frayed from being read over and over.

His room connected to a parlor filled with uninteresting furniture. Craig explained that he never used the room, preferring to spend his time sitting in the bedroom, enjoying the friends he found in books.

A door on the opposite side of the parlor opened onto another bedroom built out just like Craig's. It held a double bed and other furniture, but the bookshelves were empty.

"Whose room was this?" Landry asked, remembering Craig's discomfort when asked about a brother.

"Nobody's. I guess it was for another child. My grandfather had one child, and his father had only one who lived, so I guess it was never anyone's room. My parents never told me anything about who it was for. They didn't discuss things like that."

Landry thought it was a sad comment. The child had so little interaction with his parents that they didn't even talk about the little things in life like which ancestor occupied which room.

Craig led them back into the hall. "That's it. Let's go back and check on Joe."

"What's in those rooms?" Marty asked, pointing to the three locked doors.

"Ask all you want, Marty. They're off-limits, like I said."

As they walked downstairs, Landry considered which rooms sat above another. On the second floor just above the office was Joe's bedroom, and one of the locked rooms was on the next floor up.

The dumbwaiter shaft ran from the office to Joe's room, and then to a room they weren't allowed to go in.

Twice before he had heard the muffled sound of gears cranking inside the walls, but Craig claimed no one had used it in a long time, even though he rode in it himself.

But what if that was wrong? Landry had heard the gears moving in the walls, but what if Craig wasn't the one using the dumbwaiter?

If he didn't ride the dumbwaiter those times, who did?

CHAPTER EIGHTEEN

When they reached the first floor, Marty walked to the front door, opened it and said, "Guys, I think the weatherman nailed it. At least for us, the worst is over. Have a look."

Even in the dark they noticed how much things had improved. The rain was less intense, but the visibility gave it away. Low-hanging clouds had lifted, and for the first time since they arrived, it was possible to see all the way across the yard. It would be days before the water completely receded, but these former residents of Iberia Parish knew things would return to normal quickly.

Their optimism about the weather, the power staying on for two hours, and the possibility that tomorrow would be departure day put everyone in a better mood. They assembled in the Great Room and opened another excellent bottle of Cabernet Sauvignon from the Morisset cellar. Joe slept on the couch; Marty woke him and asked if he'd like to join them.

Joe opened his eyes and stared up at Marty. Frightened, he sat bolt upright and said, "Where am I?"

"Easy, buddy. You've been asleep. You're right here with us in Amelia House. You got a nasty bump on the head, but you'll be fine."

He looked across the room in alarm. "No! What's he doing here?" He pointed at the guys drinking wine by the fire.

"Joe, it's all right. Take it easy."

He jumped from the couch and ran toward the door. "Get me out of here! Get me away from him!"

"What's he talking about?" Alain said. "Who's he afraid of?"

Marty answered, "He's hallucinating or something, maybe because of the concussion." He took Joe's arm to guide him back to the couch, but Joe, a former Jeanerette High football star and still a strong man, jerked back and knocked Marty to the floor.

"Joe!" Alain cried, running to his side. "What is it, buddy? What's going on?"

"Him! It's him! Get me out of here!" He pointed again toward the fireplace, where only two of them now stood — Landry and Craig.

Landry understood — or thought he did. He went to Joe and said, "It's okay." Joe wasn't upset, so obviously this wasn't about Landry. There was only one man left, and Joe was afraid of him.

"He's afraid of you," Marty said to Craig. "What's that about?"

"Who knows?" Craig answered. He joined the others as Joe cowered behind Marty.

Landry watched Craig's attempt at nonchalance and Joe's unmistakable terror — and waited.

As Craig came close, Joe let out an unearthly howl and ran from the room, with Marty on his heels. In a moment they heard Marty in the kitchen trying to calm his distraught friend.

"He hurt me!" came Joe's cry from the other room.

THE EXPERIMENTS: THE BAYOU HAUNTING 5

"What's he talking about, Craig?" Landry demanded.

Craig tried to appear unconcerned, but Landry could see that he understood. "Who knows? I didn't hurt him. The doctor says he has a concussion. Looks to me like he's delusional."

"But he's not. He's terrified of you for some reason. I don't know whether you hurt him or not. None of us knows anything about what's going on."

"Neither do I."

Landry let it go, knowing Craig wouldn't reveal anything. But something had happened, and Joe was terrified of Craig now. He was two inches taller and a lot more fit than Craig, but he'd hidden behind Marty when Craig came near.

Nothing seemed to make sense, but random thoughts began to coalesce in Landry's mind. There might be a way to find the answers, but it was a risky plan that could lead to disastrous consequences. He had an idea what might be happening inside the house, and he was determined to learn the truth.

The weather had put them in a jubilant mood, but no one felt lighthearted now after what had happened with Joe. It was almost eleven anyway, and everybody except Craig walked upstairs. He stayed behind to turn off the lights and check the locks.

Since Marty's bedroom had two double beds, he suggested Joe stay in his room for the night in case he needed medical attention. Joe's switching rooms was a lucky break for Landry. If it hadn't happened, he would have had to think of another way to implement the plan he'd developed. The guys said goodnight in the hall with high hopes that tomorrow morning they'd be able to leave Iberia Parish and head home.

CHAPTER NINETEEN

The alarm on Landry's phone dinged at one thirty. He slipped on his shorts and T-shirt, tiptoed down the hall to Joe's room, and opened the door. He found the bed empty, which meant Marty and Joe were in the other room.

The dumbwaiter sat hidden in a corner identical to the one downstairs. A bookshelf stood next to the moveable panel, and a book hid the button. When he pushed it, the gears moved and then stopped. He slid the panel open, stepped into the coffin-like box and closed it. He pressed the button inside, and the car rose up the shaft.

He had a scary thought. The door was locked, and what if someone had blocked the panel so it wouldn't open either? His mind raced with an odd combination of exhilaration and dread as he tried the panel. He breathed a sigh of relief when it slid open.

In the dark room he couldn't see a thing. He paused and listened, but all was quiet, so he clicked the light on his phone and looked at the room. It was the same size as the bedroom below, but in every other way it was different. Heavy black cloths hung over the windows, allowing no light inside. It had white walls with a wainscot of stainless steel, and a tiled floor.

White steel tables and cabinets with glass doors stood against the walls. He looked at one and saw instruments similar to the ones displayed in the office. They were neatly arranged and appeared ready for use. A heavy steel table draped in white sheets stood in the middle of the room. It had restraints – heavy leather straps – on all four sides.

This was the laboratory Craig mentioned, the place his parents performed experiments. But from the setup in this room, it looked like it had been used for something else. This was an operating room.

Since the heavy curtains would keep the light both in and out, he didn't worry about turning on the lights. He flipped a switch beside the door and put his phone away. A huge surgical lamp in the center of the room illuminated the metal table with clean white light while the rest of the room was dark.

He looked at the table as thoughts ran through his mind. Coach had told him rumors of bad things happening in the house. Experiments on animals and people performed by Craig's ancestors...and his own parents.

What kinds of things happened inside these walls?

"Have you figured everything out yet?"

The voice startled him. Landry yelled and looked to where the words came from. Craig stood in shadows near the window.

"I'm trying to imagine what sorts of operations they did. Why don't you tell me?"

Craig ambled to the middle of the room and around the table toward Landry. He was in one of his fugues again, and this time he held a surgical tool — a long scalpel with a four-inch blade. Landry's eyes darted around the room. He needed an exit strategy fast.

"Hey, man," Landry said, backing away as Craig drew near. "What are you doing?"

THE EXPERIMENTS: THE BAYOU HAUNTING 5

Craig glanced behind Landry and whispered, "Hit him, Jerry!"

Landry ducked and weaved sideways, fending off a blow from behind that didn't come. He put his arms up in defense as Craig rushed him, slashing the scalpel through the air. The blade caught his shirt, ripping the sleeve. Landry feinted with his right hand and swung with his left, and his fist connected with Craig's cheekbone. He cried out, fell to the floor on his back and was still.

Landry ensured there was no one behind him before kneeling to check on Craig. He didn't notice a vapor arise from a dark corner. It floated toward them and an eerie sound — a mixture of rushing wind and mournful groans — seemed to emanate from the mist itself.

As Landry sat on the floor beside Craig, the vapor swirled around the metal table and the anguished sighs grew louder. He watched it, poised to move if it drew closer.

Noticing Craig's eyes were closed, Landry shook him and asked if he was okay.

Craig opened his eyes. "What...what happened?" The blow had jolted him back to reality, and as Craig sat up, the strange vapor evaporated.

"You came at me with this." Landry picked up the scalpel and showed it to Craig. "I hit you in the jaw and you fell."

Craig put his hand to his face and winced. "Have you done much boxing?" he asked with a feeble smile.

Landry admitted that was the first time he'd ever hit someone.

Craig wanted to know what happened.

Although Craig had some explaining to do himself, Landry started first. He couldn't explain his presence here except by telling the truth.

"You may not like what I have to say, but I don't care. You've acted so odd that I decided to look around on my own. I wanted to see where the dumbwaiter went on the third floor, so I rode it. That's the how and why of it. I've only known you for three days, but several times you faded from reality. Sometimes you're not aware of it, but everyone else damn sure is. It's happened over and over since Thursday night, and it happened here just before I hit you.

"I thought I was alone, but you stood there by the window. You came at me with a scalpel and sliced my sleeve."

"Looks like I sliced more than that," Craig said, pointing to a rivulet of blood that ran down Landry's right arm. The slash that cut his T-shirt had also grazed the skin. "I'm sorry, Landry. I wasn't aware of what I was doing."

"That's not all. You glanced behind me and told someone named Jerry to hit me. I ducked, you slashed, and I decked you. Who's Jerry?"

He paused just long enough for Landry to know he was thinking what to say. "No idea. I told you I wasn't aware I did any of that, and I don't know anyone named Jerry."

Landry knew that was a lie, but when it came down to it, this wasn't Landry's business. Craig could say and do whatever he pleased. He was in his own house, it was his life, and he didn't have to answer for anything. Regardless, Landry had to figure this out. His frequent withdrawals, the odd way he acted at the cemetery, something about a mysterious brother, and this bizarre operating room — all of it tied together somehow.

Landry stood and helped Craig up. He looked around the room and said, "I guess this is the house laboratory you talked about. What did your folks use that operating table for?"

Landry's comment struck a nerve. Craig snapped, "Quit calling them my *folks*. My great-grandfather built this house. I already told you they were doctors, so why shouldn't they have a room like this? Why do you keep bugging me about it?"

"Right. And you said your father played the stock market."

Craig nodded.

"So he never used this room, I guess. What about your mother? Was she a stay-at-home mom? Did she ever come in here?" Landry knew this was uncharted territory. He had triggered Craig's anger earlier at the mausoleum, but now he was angry himself. He wanted answers.

Craig said, "You can't write about what happened here. This room is off the record."

"Oh no you don't. We're not going through this again. My own experiences are one hundred percent on the record and you damn well know it. I'm free to disclose my observations about everything I see. Now tell me about this place. What kind of work did they do in here?"

There arose a low moan that amplified a hundredfold within seconds, reverberating throughout the room in a crescendo of pitiful wailing. It was nothing like the earlier sounds. It was like being in a movie theater where thumping bass sounds emanate from every corner, creating a palpable vibration that fills a person's mind with dread and impending danger.

Landry said, "What's that?"

"I don't know what you're talking about."

Landry pointed here and there. "Those noises. Those awful sounds coming from everywhere. It's like people are in excruciating pain."

"What would you know about excruciating pain?" Craig said, his tone of voice becoming threatening. "You never even hit anyone before." He turned and stared at something across the room, over in that corner where the strange vapor had arisen moments ago.

"Are you there?" Craig whispered, and the moans grew stronger. Landry had never heard anything like them — it was as if the sound itself was swirling everywhere, building toward an ear-splitting crescendo that resounded with horror and suffering.

Craig had spoken to someone in a dark corner across the room, but was anyone there? Ignoring his fear of impending danger, Landry ran across the room. By God, this time he was going to get answers.

The overhead light went out. He switched on his phone and fumbled for flashlight mode, and then he sensed something moving very close to him. The weeping and groaning reached new heights as he took a few steps backwards, hit something solid, and felt a gossamer veil slide across his face. The moans and wails became more focused as his fingers at last found the flashlight button. He was alone in the middle of the room beside the operating table, and he sensed that the table itself was what triggered the horrific wails of pain.

Then there was nothing. No words, no thoughts, no sounds.

Nothing at all.

CHAPTER TWENTY

"Wake up, Landry. Wake up!"

Someone was shaking him so hard that his head banged against the floor.

He opened his eyes and found Marty and Alain kneeling beside him.

"Where...where am I?"

"Where do you think you are?" Marty said, fishing to learn how much he recalled.

"In the house. Is that right?"

"Yes. It's two a.m. I heard some loud bumps, came out into the hall, and found you here. You're on the floor at the bottom of the stairway. You woke Alain up too. It looks like you fell down the stairs. You went to the third floor, I guess."

Memories returned. Craig had turned off the lights and struck him with something.

Did he drag me to the stairway and throw me down?

He'd heard anguished cries from everywhere in the room. Maybe Craig didn't hit him. If not, how did he get here without knowing it?

They helped Landry stand, and Alain asked if he might have been sleepwalking.

He had to learn more before engaging in speculation, so he created a story. "I couldn't sleep, so I went to check things out. Sometimes I get myself into trouble poking around old houses in the middle of the night. I went upstairs to try those locked doors again. When I came back, I must have fallen down the stairs in the dark."

"Now there are two of you with head injuries," Marty said with a grin. "I'm supposed to be off duty. This is my reunion weekend, but I've played doctor the entire time."

"It's a good thing you're here," Landry said, and he meant it.

"What's that noise?" Alain said as the quiet sound of gears began again. Landry recognized it at once. Craig was in the dumbwaiter.

"Guys, I'm exhausted. I'm going to the kitchen to get a bottle of water, and then it's off to bed for me. See you guys tomorrow."

They returned to their bedrooms as he walked downstairs and went into the office. Craig stood by the fireplace, staring into the dying embers, unaware of Landry's presence until he spoke.

"It's time to talk, Craig. What's going on here? You can help me, or I can do this on my own. Either way, it's not a secret anymore. If you'd like any input on how I present your story, I suggest you tell me everything. Otherwise I'm going with what I know and saw."

Craig spoke without turning around. "I should never have come back. I knew something might happen, but I decided one visit couldn't hurt. I had to go to the ceremony at St. Anne's, so what was the harm in attending my class reunion? I told myself I'd come to Jeanerette, but I wouldn't come to the house. I should have known better, because I know the powers they have. When I was at the hotel, something drew me to the crypt. Not something —

them. *They* commanded me to come to Jeanerette and I obeyed. I went to the cemetery, and then they forced me to come here."

"Who are *they*?"

"*They* are Frank and Maria and my grandfather Albert, and his father, Marco. It's the lot of them — my entire family. They..." He paused and cocked his head.

"Listen!"

There was that sound again. The dumbwaiter. But who —?

Craig turned and stared at Landry for the first time. He was wide-eyed and his voice changed to a monotone.

"Who's in it, Craig?"

He paused a moment and cocked his head, listening.

"They forbid me to tell you anything, and they forbid you to write the story. Do you understand?"

"No, I don't. Explain it to me."

"I warned you." Like a wooden soldier, Craig marched across the room to the panel and opened it. A whirling vapor swept from the dumbwaiter and enveloped him. It rose up and around his body, wrapping him in an opaque mist swirling with colors. As it enveloped him like a cocoon, he screamed, "Stop it! Why are you doing this to me? I'm doing what you ask!"

From inside the cocoon came an ethereal sigh, a drawn-out moan that seemed to last forever. Sensations of sadness and regret permeated the room as Landry ran to help Craig. Approaching the swirling mass that wrapped Craig from head to toe, he saw the vapors were now tendrils, weaving and interlocking with each other to draw the mist into a viselike grip around his body.

When he struck out at the vapor, he found it wasn't a tangible thing. It was a cloud — something seen but not felt. Instead of hitting the tendrils, his fist entered the foggy haze and connected with Craig's side. He collapsed and the vapor disintegrated.

Landry ran toward the hall to shout for the others, but he shrank back in alarm as he watched the vapor reform in the doorway, blocking his path. Its color was darker now — a stormy gray instead of white — and its filmy vines extended toward him. He backed away, but tripped on the rug and fell.

As the mist swathed him in tendrils that seemed intangible but bound him tighter and tighter, faces were the last things Landry saw. Men and women, all with mouths agape and uttering pitiful wails that he sensed rather than heard. Then other faces appeared, the faces of a man and woman wearing white lab coats that swirled through the mist. He knew those people.

Those two were the perpetrators, the ones who made the others scream in misery. They were the ones who lured Craig back to the house.

Those were his mother and father.

CHAPTER TWENTY-ONE

Ten days later

Landry opened his eyes and looked around, wondering where he was. He lay in a bed with side rails, and a tube ran from his hand to a plastic bag hanging on a stand. This place seemed like a hospital, although the room looked more like one in an Embassy Suites than a cookie-cutter hospital room.

A lady in a white jacket walked through the door. "You're awake! Great!" As she checked a monitor beside his bed, he asked where he was.

"You're in Villemont Clinic. Wait a moment and I'll be right back. Someone has been waiting for you." She left the room for a moment, and he smiled when she returned with his girlfriend, Cate, who rushed to his side.

"My God, Landry! I've been so worried about you!"

"How about a hug?" he said, and they held each other for a long moment.

"I thought you were in London.

Cate laughed. "Doctor, I'd say his memory's just fine." To Landry she replied, "You're right. I was in London when I learned about your...accident. I came as soon as I could."

"She's been here every day, Mr. Drake," the doctor added. "She's been waiting for you to wake up ever since..." She paused.

"Ever since what? What were you about to say?"

"Ever since they brought you in. Dr. Scorza took you to University Hospital in New Orleans first, and they transferred you here."

"Dr. Scorza? Who's he? And where's here? What's Villemont Clinic? Where am I, and why am I here?"

Cate realized Landry's memory wasn't so good after all.

The doctor said, "Let me check you over for a minute, and I'll leave you two alone so Cate can fill in the missing parts of the puzzle." She checked his vital signs, entered them in an iPad, and left.

Cate showed Landry how to elevate the top part of his bed and pulled a chair over. "Let's start with what you know," she said, "and I'll tell you what I can about the rest."

"I know who I am, where I work, where I live, who you are — all that stuff. What else do you want to know?"

"Do you remember going to Iberia Parish to interview Craig Morisset?"

"Sure. We spent the weekend together. He acted strange sometimes, and because of the hurricane, five of us ended up spending Saturday night at his house." He looked out the window and noticed blue clouds in the sky and a sunny day. "Looks nice outside; I guess the storm's over. No, wait. That's not possible unless...where am I? Am I still in Louisiana?"

"Yes, you're in Chalmette. Do you know where it is?"

"Why are you asking me stupid questions? Chalmette's just outside New Orleans. The doctor said I'm at Villemont Clinic. What is that?"

She paused a moment. "I want to talk to you more before we get into where you are. Keep telling me what you recall."

"No, Cate. You tell me. Where am I?"

"Okay. You're at a private hospital called Villemont Clinic. You've been here for ten days."

"Are you serious? I've been unconscious for ten days?"

"Sort of. You've been in and out, but Dr. Wallace said once you woke up, it might take time to reconstruct your short-term memory. It's nothing to be worried about."

"This doesn't look like any hospital I've been in before." He was about to ask what kind of facility it was, but her last answer gave him a clue.

"Reconstruct my short-term memory? What kind of doctor is Dr. Wallace?"

"Villemont's a private psychiatric hospital, Landry."

"So she's a shrink," he muttered. "I'm in the nuthouse."

"You've been through an ordeal, and this is the best place for you to recover."

"What kind of ordeal have I been through? I've been lying here for ten days and didn't know it."

"Okay, mister know-it-all. Do you want to figure this out, or do you want to shut up a minute and let me help you?"

He smiled and took her hand. "Having you here is wonderful, Cate. It's been a long time and I'm so glad you came, even if you insist on bitching at me."

She laughed, happy he still had his sense of humor. "I came the minute I heard. Switching plans took almost two days. I flew to Houston and I came here the next morning. But enough about that. We were rebuilding your memory. You went to Craig Morisset's house in Jeanerette on Saturday. What happened?"

"I remember a man named Joe...Joe somebody. He got hit in the eye or had a concussion or something. Marty...aha, I remember! That's who Dr. Scorza is! Marty!

Dr. Wallace said he took me to University Hospital. That makes sense; Marty was at the house too. So how did I get from University to the funny farm?"

"Stop it. It's already obvious that keeping you on track won't be easy, but that's my job. I'm the official memory rebuilder and you're my patient. Obey orders, Mr. Drake."

"Okay, have it your way. You owe me big time for this, just so you know. We had dinner at the house, and we looked at a dumbwaiter. Wait a second, that's something important. Amelia House has a kind of elevator that runs from…let's see. It runs from an office to a bedroom — Joe's bedroom — on the second floor. Then it goes on up. At least I think it does. I rode it." He paused. "Do I? Yeah, I'm sure I did."

She watched Landry stare off into the distance as if the thoughts he needed were sitting out there somewhere, just waiting for him to retrieve them. He started a sentence, then stopped and started again. Bits and pieces repositioned themselves in his mind, but she could see how difficult it was for him, and it made her sad.

"Some kind of operating room is on the third floor. A room where bad things happened. Craig's ancestors were doctors. They did experiments or something. But it makes no sense that I'd know that. Those rooms were locked — right? Weren't some of the rooms locked? Was I in that room, or is it my imagination?"

"Only you can say. Try to remember."

He sat up, knitted his brow and closed his eyes. He was trying, struggling to bring things together that should be easy to remember. But now it wasn't working. He ground his fist into his palm in frustration, and a chime by the bed dinged.

A nurse ran into the room, looked at a reading on a machine, and silenced the alarm. She took a hypodermic bottle and a syringe from her pocket. As she pulled on

THE EXPERIMENTS: THE BAYOU HAUNTING 5

rubber gloves, Dr. Wallace came in, and the nurse showed her Landry's blood pressure reading.

"We've had enough chatting for now," the doctor said as the nurse injected medicine into his IV tube. "He's been through a lot — more than we even know, I'm sure — and it's time for him to rest."

Landry heard most of her words, but the last few were echoes from somewhere far, far away as he drifted off into a peaceful sleep.

He awoke with someone holding his hand. It was a nice feeling — not as nice as the blissful slumber that was fading away, but someone he cared for was next to him, holding his hand.

"Hi," Cate said as he opened his eyes. "Welcome back."

"Nice to be here," he mumbled. "How long was I gone this time?"

"Almost four hours. You needed rest. I pushed you too hard and I'm sorry." He brushed away a tear that ran down her cheek. "I thought I'd lost you, that's all. I was afraid you might not come back, and I couldn't imagine what I'd do without you."

He pulled her close and held her in his arms. "You're not going to lose me, even if you wanted to. It's killing me that I can't remember what happened yesterday — not yesterday, but ten days ago. That blows my mind. It seems like yesterday I was…"

He paused, struggled to recall something, and she said he should quit trying so hard. "It'll come back to you. Physically you're in great shape. Something happened at Craig's house, and you'll remember it before long."

"I did go to that locked room — the laboratory. Someone else was there too. It was dark, but the storm was almost over. It was night and I rode the dumbwaiter up to see what was there. But someone caught me."

"Enough of that for today. Let's talk about other things instead of that. Where do you work? Who's your boss?"

"Come on. Piece of cake. I work at Channel 9 in the Quarter. Ted Carpenter's my boss, and I'll bet he's about to have a cow over me being gone."

"Not at all. He checks in a lot, and I called him this afternoon to let him know you were awake. He'll come see you when they allow it."

"I'm not allowed to see people? Am I on lockdown?"

She laughed. "It sounds like you're remembering the old asylum at Victory. Remember the *Bayou Hauntings* episode you did called 'Forgotten Men'? I was with you when it happened. I was scared to death. Do you remember that?"

"Yes, clearly. My long-term memory's fine, I guess. I'm worried about the things that happened yesterday. I don't mean yesterday, but ten days ago. Those are gone."

Smoothly, she switched subjects. "I'm hungry. Would you like to go down and get something to eat?"

"Are the inmates allowed to leave their cells?"

She cackled. "Ha ha. Yeah, you felons are allowed to eat. It's the humane thing to do, after all. You've been fed intravenously since you got here. I'm surprised you aren't starving to death."

"Now that you mention it, I am a little hungry. I hope this place doesn't have hospital food."

She went to the closet and tossed him a sweatshirt and pants that she'd brought over from his apartment a few days ago. "I was just waiting for you to wake up and get dressed," she said, helping him out of the hospital pajamas.

"How about you jump in bed with me?" he said when he was naked. That made her laugh again, and she said there would be plenty of time for that later. She asked if he needed a wheelchair, and he emphatically refused.

They strolled down a wide hallway with lots of windows and cheery paintings on the walls. The people

THE EXPERIMENTS: THE BAYOU HAUNTING 5

they passed — some who clearly worked there and others who might have been patients or maybe visitors — all spoke and smiled.

The dining room was spacious and airy and looked more like an Italian restaurant than a hospital facility. She asked if he wanted to sit on the patio, and he said yes. In a moment they were seated, and he was pleasantly surprised when a waiter came over and asked if he wanted to see the wine list.

"Bring it on," Landry replied enthusiastically. "I'll be damned, Cate. That Dr. Wallace must not be such a bad gal if she'll let me have alcohol. How ab out a vodka tonic?"

"The wine list's for me," Cate said with a smile. "Your doctor says you're on too many meds for alcohol just yet."

She ordered a glass of Pinot Grigio, they split a Caesar salad, and he had a twelve-ounce filet mignon. Although he couldn't finish it, he declared it the best thing he'd ever eaten. Afterwards they shared a hot fudge sundae.

"That was a great meal," he said as he pushed back from the table. "I'm exhausted. I guess ten days of bed rest wasn't enough. By the way, I forgot to ask where you're staying."

"At your place. I hoped you wouldn't mind."

"I wonder how soon I can go home. I'd love to be there right now with you."

"You'll get better every day. I'm just glad you're awake; Dr. Wallace kept my spirits up and she was right. My old Landry is back."

"Right now I feel like your really, really old Landry," he said with a yawn and a stretch. "I think I'll take a wheelchair back to my room. I'm ready for bed."

CHAPTER TWENTY-TWO

Landry had been comatose when Marty brought him to University Hospital that Sunday morning, and Marty knew little about what had happened to the well-known TV personality. He told the ER physician Landry fell down a flight of stairs and hit his head. When he went downstairs for water, Marty and the others returned to bed. The next morning one of them found Landry unconscious in an office. Marty speculated he might have suffered a seizure after a concussion, but he wasn't certain of anything.

The hospital needed someone who could act on Landry's behalf. A clerk called his employer, WCCY-TV, where Ted advised he had a mother somewhere back East, but they should contact his fiancée, Cate Adams. He gave them her number.

Cate wasn't engaged to Landry, but they'd discussed it enough times that she might as well have been. When she got the call, she left London, flew to New Orleans, and met with his physician. At his direction, she signed the paperwork that moved Landry to Villemont Clinic for evaluation and treatment when he regained consciousness.

Landry's psychiatrist, Dr. Wallace, called Marty to hear his account of what had happened to her patient. She asked if he had been drinking on the night he fell down the stairs. Did he have a history of blackouts or mental issues?

Marty repeated what he'd told the doctors at University Hospital. He'd met Landry three days earlier and knew nothing about his history. Yes, the four of them were drinking that night, but Landry and Craig had consumed far less than he and Alain.

Dr. Wallace said the information sent over from the New Orleans hospital showed Landry was drug- and alcohol-free at the time of admission. Given the timeframe involved, that made sense to Marty. They went to bed at eleven, he found Landry at the bottom of the stairs at two, and Alain found him unconscious in the office around eight the next morning. Between packing up and slow driving on flooded highways, Marty hadn't arrived at University Hospital with his unconscious patient until around noon. By then no alcohol would remain in his bloodstream.

Marty had nothing else to add, and it took ten days before Landry awoke and began to piece together the details.

———

Landry sat with Cate in a gazebo that overlooked a small lake. Dr. Wallace urged her to keep encouraging him to recall that night at Amelia House, and he erupted with frustration each time his mind wouldn't give him the answers he wanted.

"I have an idea," Landry said. "I want to talk to Craig Morisset and learn what he remembers about that night." The moment he uttered the words, a flash of recollection flew into his mind. Something bad. A dark room filled with medical equipment. An operating theater. Yesterday he recalled the room, but now there was more. He'd stood in that room along with Craig. Someone was in pain — there came mournful cries from someone strapped to a table. In the darkness someone swung at him.

Who? Craig?

Saying nothing, Cate watched him put the pieces back together in his mind. He was concentrating, giving it everything he had as he attempted to weave the tapestry. She waited to speak until his facial muscles relaxed and his shoulders sagged.

"Did you come up with something new?"

"Possibly. There's an operating room or something upstairs. I was there and so was Craig. Someone hit me — was it him? It had to be; no one else was there. But wait...he was talking to someone behind me. Who was it? I wonder if that person hit me."

"Do you have Craig's number? Should we call him?"

"I have it, but there's something about him that bothers me. Right now, I'll call Marty Scorza instead. Let's find out what he knows."

Cate was aware of Dr. Wallace's conversation with Marty, but she didn't mention it. It was better for Landry to use his mind than for her to give him clues. "Okay, let's do it. What's his number?"

Landry recalled that he practiced medicine in Atlanta. With that, Cate found his office number, and a receptionist took her message.

She asked Landry leading questions that might elicit memories. "Where did you stay those nights you spent in New Iberia?" she asked, and he answered at once. He also recalled sitting in the bar that first afternoon and attending the Cajun Cavalry's reunion party, where he met both Marty and Craig.

"The next morning I drove to Jeanerette. It was crazy; the evacuees' cars were bumper-to-bumper on the northbound side. I drove to my old house and I wish I hadn't. We had a small place, but Mom made it beautiful inside and out. Now it's one of a row of shanties on our street. It made me sad."

"What did you do after that?"

"I made donuts all morning."

Cate smiled and shook her head. "I don't think so, honey. I'll bet you're remembering another time. You didn't make donuts all morning during a hurricane."

"You think I'm crazy, don't you? But I'm not, because I really did make donuts." He laughed, and he told her about helping out in his old coach's shop. She laughed too and praised him for remembering.

His phone rang and an unfamiliar number appeared. He answered.

"Marty! Seems like only yesterday I saw you." And he meant it. To him, it felt like a day ago instead of eleven.

He told Marty where he was and his progression so far, and Marty told him details about the night he fell. He didn't remember it — lying at the bottom of the stairs, going back to bed, turning up unconscious the next morning in the office, or being transported back to New Orleans.

"You saw my head. I wonder if someone hit me. I have a vague recollection about being in a laboratory on the third floor."

"Somebody might have hit you, but your mind's playing tricks on you about that laboratory. Craig gave us a tour — remember? He showed us some bedrooms, but there were three locked rooms he refused to open. Nobody but Craig knows what's inside them. Does any of this ring a bell?"

Cate watched Landry's face light up as more memories returned. "Yeah, I recall all of that. I remember a dumbwaiter too. Am I right?"

"Yes. Craig showed us how it worked. He rode it up one floor, but he wouldn't let us. Good remembering."

"I have to go back there, Marty. I have to face things — to walk through the house and see if my memory comes back." He glanced at Cate, who sat staring into her lap and shaking her head. "Will you go with me?"

His request struck Marty as an imposition. He was a busy physician, and a person he hardly knew wanted him to drop everything and go back to Louisiana. He'd done enough. He'd taken Landry to the hospital, after all. What else did this guy expect?

"I'm a little busy. Perhaps you've forgotten I'm a doctor. I see patients all day long. I don't have time to come back to Louisiana. Why don't you ask Craig? He sits around on a yacht all day. I'll bet he can help you." He said he had to go, wished Landry a speedy recovery, and disconnected.

Landry glanced at Cate. "From the look on your face, I take it you're not happy that I want to go back to Jeanerette."

"You can't go right now. It wouldn't be good for you. It might happen sometime later, but not this soon. I'll guarantee Dr. Wallace will agree with me. What did Marty say when you asked him to go with you?"

"He blew me off. He said he's too busy. I was around him long enough to realize he's a self-centered egotist. He's not interested in helping me. He told me to call Craig."

"He's right. You can't just go waltzing into his house without his permission, so you have to call him sometime. That's presuming Dr. Wallace and I let you go back."

"*Let* me? What are you all — my keepers? Oh, never mind. I forgot where I am. You all think I'm crazy."

"Come on, Landry. That's not funny. You aren't crazy — you suffered some kind of traumatic event. You have short-term amnesia, but I'm impressed how quickly things are coming back. Did your talk with Marty help?"

"No. He says I'm mistaken about a laboratory in the house. Marty didn't see one, so neither could I have because three rooms were locked. I'm certain that laboratory has something to do with all this, but I just can't recall what it is. And you're right. I have to call Craig because I can't go inside without his permission. He hasn't known me any longer than Marty has, but I hope he'll agree to help me."

He paused as a memory blossomed in his brain.

"There's something different about Craig. A few times he acted very strange and fell into some kind of trance. He was there with us, but he wasn't, if that makes sense." He paused as another memory arrived in his mental inbox. "I saw him at the cemetery in Jeanerette. He was zoned out in front of his family's mausoleum. And again at his house. I saw him there too."

That didn't surprise Cate. "Before you went up to Iberia Parish, you told me about Craig's parents. They burned to death in a fire, but he never came home or even gave them a funeral. He's got big problems in his head, if you ask me. No wonder he zoned out when he was back in his hometown. He kept his family house just as it was on the day they died, and he didn't come back for seventeen years. When you saw him in the cemetery, his mind had to be spinning with thoughts. Maybe it was regret, or maybe sadness or even joy. Who knows? The only thing certain is that memories would have flooded his mind."

He knew the trances Craig experienced weren't the same as recalling an experience in the past, but there was no reason to keep discussing it. He started to place the call when a hazy recollection swam through his mind.

Don't call Craig. It's a bad idea to ask his permission to return. Landry couldn't remember why that might be. He felt just the opposite. Maybe going back and unlocking those doors on the top floor would unlock the portal in his mind that held the rest of his memories.

Before she could object, he made the call. He reached voicemail and left a message, although he doubted Craig would call back. He'd think Landry was hard at work crafting a story about Amelia House and the eccentric tech millionaire, and he'd want nothing to do with it.

Every morning Landry met with Dr. Wallace, and today Cate walked him to her office. She gave the doctor a brief update on Landry, the call with Marty, and how his memory rebuilding was progressing. Then she asked if they could leave the property for lunch. "I thought getting back on familiar ground might be a positive thing," she added. At that, Landry perked up and asked if she was taking him to Jeanerette. Cate started to laugh, but realized he wasn't joking.

"Talk to the doctor about Jeanerette," Cate said. "Get her opinion about your going back to Amelia House. Meanwhile, how about it, Doc? Any chance we can make a quick trip to New Orleans?"

She agreed, reminding Landry not to drink because of his medications. "You have my number," she told Cate. "Call if you have any problems, and please have him back by three. He goes to the gym with a trainer at three, so he can keep those muscles strong."

When the appointment ended, they walked to the parking lot and climbed into the Jeep. "Lunch is on me," she said, and asked where he'd like to eat. He picked Irene's, a cozy Italian place on Bienville she hadn't been to. On the drive in, he asked how the Jeep had gotten back from Jeanerette, since Marty had brought him to the hospital.

"I hired a tow truck to pick it up," she said with a grin. "You owe me two hundred bucks."

"Put it on my account. I'll owe you a lot more before all this is over."

They selected a table in the window. When they had their menus, she said, "We have so many great go-to places in the Quarter, I'm surprised you picked someplace new." She wondered if it was because reviving the memories scared him.

"I picked it because we've never been here together. Wherever we eat in the Quarter, we sit at the bar, talk to our friend the bartender, linger over a glass of wine or two, and then have our meal. And we go to the same few places. There's no alcohol for me today, so I chose someplace unfamiliar. I don't want your sultry smile and your enchanting eyes to tempt me. Oh, and by the way, I love the food here," he explained, saying the oysters Irene were to die for.

"Oh boy." She laughed. "It's getting a little deep in here. But I get it. Today's not the day to sip wine and talk to the bartender, and that's what we always do. Makes perfect sense."

They had a quiet lunch that she proclaimed one of the best in town, and he was glad she liked the venue. When the waiter brought the check, Landry automatically reached for his wallet and then said, "I guess you really are taking me to lunch. That damned doctor stole my money." She laughed and put her credit card on the table as his phone rang.

"Craig, it's good to hear from you. I hoped you'd return my call."

"How are you feeling? Last time I saw you, Marty was loading you up to go to the hospital."

"Okay, all things considered." Without going into detail about things, he said he was experiencing some amnesia about that weekend, and he had a favor to ask. "I believe going back to Amelia House might reset my memory. I want to be there and experience it again. Something happened to me there — I'm not sure what, but I need to find out. Would you be willing to meet me there?"

Craig apologized that he didn't have time to go back to Louisiana. Like Marty's turndown, Craig's didn't surprise Landry either. Landry remembered some of the issues Craig had with his family and the house. And he recalled that Craig sometimes went into a trance. He wondered if the demons that plagued Craig's mind were what drove him to escape from reality.

"I wish I could help you," Craig said.

"If you're serious, then there is something you can do. Allow me to go to the house myself."

"We've been through this before. I refuse to let you portray Amelia House as another of your haunted showplaces. It's my home..."

Certain this might be his last chance to see the house, he used every memory he could conjure up.

"It's your home only because you grew up there. Until the other day you hadn't been back since 2003. You have no sentimental attachment to that house or to your family. When you returned at last, unusual things happened to you. They happened to me too. You know what I'm talking about. I'm convinced there's something at Amelia House you don't want me to find out about.

"You call your parents the people who birthed you. The bitterness is impossible to miss, Craig. There's a story here and I'm willing to cast things in the best light. I want to go there with your blessing, but if you refuse, I'll do the story anyway. There's going to be a show about Amelia House, and I'll reveal every strange thing I saw. You can't stop me from revealing the secrets now. It's down to this: you're either with me, or you're against me. It's your choice and I want an answer now."

The line went dead. Landry called back, but the call went to voicemail.

"He hung up on me."

Cate said, "Really? How surprising, given how cordial you were. I don't know this guy, but you gave it to him pretty hard. Do you think that attitude's going to win him over?"

"It was my last shot. Maybe he'll listen to something I said."

"Yeah, especially that 'you're either with me or against me' part. That would endear me to you forever."

A little irritated by her attitude, Landry shrugged. "I did what I thought best. Let's go."

Craig's call had darkened his mood. On the way back he seemed lost in thought. She wondered if memories were coming back, or if he was just thinking how to change Craig's mind.

He told Cate she was off duty for the evening. "I'm already tired, and I'll be exhausted after physical therapy. You don't have to hang around with me. Go do something fun."

"I'll do whatever you say, Landry. Having a free night in the Quarter by myself isn't my idea of fun, and I know you'd rather be home than at Villemont. But if you've had enough of me for now, I'll respect that and leave you alone."

"That's not what I meant. It's not fair to expect you to babysit me. Oh, I need to tell you that I asked Dr. Wallace when she was going to release me."

It bothered her he hadn't mentioned it earlier. "Is that right? Were you planning to tell me sometime?"

"Lighten up, okay? This is hard for me, and you're starting to twist around everything I say right now."

"In case you don't know it, this is hard for me too, Landry. Tell me what the doctor said."

"She said my memory before and after those four days is fine. My bump on the head wasn't a concussion. From a physical standpoint, all's well. She wants me to stay a few more days. She wants to try some mental exercises to see if she can fill in the blanks. If not, I'll go home and we'll see how it goes from there. I want to get back to work. With or without Craig's help, I'm doing a *Bayou Hauntings* show about Amelia House."

Cate parked under the porte cochere at Villemont Clinic and walked inside with him. He asked why she didn't park in the lot, and she said she was doing what he suggested. "You came out of a coma yesterday, you scared the hell out of me, and you're being evaluated for memory lapses. I cut my trip to Europe short and came here to sit by your bed for ten days. I cried and worried and called your name and stuck a straw in your mouth, hoping you'd suck a little water, and when you didn't, I cried some more. I know this has been pure hell for you. But it's been the same for me, and I don't think you realize it.

"You're upset with me because you're frustrated with yourself. You can't remember fast enough, and you're taking it out on me. You told me to hit the road, and I think for a while that might be a good thing for both of us. Until you're ready for me to intrude on your life again, I'm going home."

"Just to New Orleans, right? I want you to come back tomorrow."

"No. I'm going back to Galveston."

"Don't leave, Cate," he said, but she squeezed his arm and said it was all right.

"You need space. We both hate hospitals. You're frustrated because of what you're going through, and you need some time alone to figure things out." She kissed him, put her finger to his lips when he tried to protest, and walked out.

At seven thirty that evening Craig called him back.

CHAPTER TWENTY-THREE

The next morning, he asked his doctor if he was free to leave.

"Anytime," she replied. "You're here voluntarily. As I mentioned yesterday, I'd like a few more days to try other things, but only if you agree. What are you thinking?"

He told her what he had in mind, and she asked what Cate thought about his plans.

"She doesn't know about them. She left yesterday, Dr. Wallace. In fact, I imagine you already know that. She called you, didn't she?"

"Yes. We spoke yesterday after she dropped you off. She cares very much for you, Landry, and I'm sure you know that. She was terrified that you'd never wake up, but she stayed by your side until you did. Everybody needs a rock now and then, even TV personalities who think they're superheroes. Who else do you have to confide in? When you're scared or lonely or excited, who listens while you talk things through?"

He admitted that everything Dr. Wallace was saying made sense. Cate was the only person he had ever let into his heart and mind. She was the only one who understood who he was and why he did crazy things sometimes.

"So will you tell her your plans? I'm asking because I think you haven't thought through your idea. You've decided what you want to do, but your mind's in a fragile state, whether you admit it or not. I'd like a few more days with you, but I can't stop you from leaving."

He promised he'd call Cate. He just didn't promise when.

That afternoon Landry took Lyft to his apartment and dropped off his things from the hospital. Then he walked to the garage on Governor Nicholls Street to confirm Cate had dropped off the Jeep.

Landry called his cameraman Phil Vandegriff, explained what he was doing, and told him what he needed. "Let me go with you," Phil begged, but Landry said it wasn't possible. He'd promised the owner he would be alone.

Phil said he'd go by the station, gather the equipment, and meet him at ten the next morning. "Keep this between us," Landry said. "Ted doesn't know yet. I'll call him sometime tomorrow."

Landry spent a comfortable night in his own bed, rose around eight, packed a few things, and picked up the Jeep. He parked on Decatur and walked to Café du Monde, where Phil was digging into a plate of beignets. They went to the car and spent twenty minutes going through two duffels. Phil brought out cameras, tripods, a video recorder and other equipment he used in Landry's paranormal investigations. He showed him everything, wished him well, and left for work.

Once he was outside New Orleans and heading toward Morgan City, Landry called his boss. He owed Ted an explanation about what he was up to, because Ted deserved to know. Telling his boss where he was headed also might help him if problems arose.

THE EXPERIMENTS: THE BAYOU HAUNTING 5

He omitted some key parts of the story. He didn't mention that he'd discharged himself from the clinic, or that he threatened to expose Craig's bizarre behavior if he didn't cooperate. He also didn't admit how little he still recalled about that weekend at Amelia House.

What he did say was that Craig consented to Landry's going to the house alone, he planned to spend the night there, and he'd be in touch when he had something to report.

Craig had said a caretaker would meet him at the house. He couldn't give Landry a name because his management company would send whoever was available. Per their agreement, Landry had just twenty-four hours, and he'd tell Craig everything he experienced. Some or all of it might become part of the Amelia House documentary — that was part of the deal — and he agreed there would be no surprises. Craig couldn't vet the material Landry used, but he did have the right to see it before the public.

Landry turned onto the old highway in Patterson and entered Jeanerette from the south. He crossed Bayside Street and turned down the long drive to Amelia House. The water that overflowed from Bayou Teche had given the lawn a good soaking. Now it was lush and green.

There were no vehicles at the house, and he wondered if the caretaker had gotten the message. Finding the back door locked, he knocked several times. A tall man in his fifties wearing a pair of bib overalls answered the door. "Morning. I'm Gerald Oubre. You must be Landry Drake."

"Were you here when Craig and several of us rode out the storm?" The man didn't look familiar, but a lot of blanks remained in Landry's brain about those four days.

"No, sir. I live down in Calumet, and when it started raining hard, I took my wife and kids and packed 'em in the car. She has a sister in Opelousas. Took us hours to get there, but we made it."

"Did your house take a hit?"

"It's on stilts, thank God. There would have been two feet of water in the house otherwise. But enough about me. What can I help you unload?"

"I can get it. It's not much." He wished Phil could have come along — his photographic expertise and an extra pair of eyes would have come in handy — but a deal was a deal. He brought in the duffels and his backpack, dumping everything in the office.

"Are you staying?" he asked Gerald, who said he could do that if Landry wanted, but he'd been told to get Landry situated, leave and return at the same time tomorrow to lock things up. That was fine with Landry; he didn't want someone taking notes about every move he made.

Landry said, "When I drove in, I didn't see a car, so I wondered if you were here. Where'd you park?"

"My truck's in the shop. I hitched a ride to the bridge and walked from there. Can I give you my number so if you need something, you can call me?"

"Sure." Landry put it in his phone and said goodbye. The man's story didn't ring true, but he had work to do. He needed Gerald to leave more than he wanted to learn why he made up a story about his truck.

Through the window he watched the caretaker walk to the road and head south toward the drawbridge. Once he was out of sight, Landry walked into the office, which would be his base of operations. He unpacked everything, ran extension cords, and tested each piece of equipment. Then he took a brief walk through the house.

As he walked down the second-floor hallway, he looked into the open rooms on both sides. Guest bedrooms, he remembered. Everyone had stayed on this floor. *No, not all of us. Craig stayed somewhere else. There were four of us. Landry, Marty, Joe and...*

Four, right? Or even more? What were the others' names?

Dammit, why can't I remember?

THE EXPERIMENTS: THE BAYOU HAUNTING 5

The bedrooms on one side of the hallway overlooked the back of the house. They'd used ones on the opposite side. He remembered the tall French doors that opened onto a porch and overlooked the Teche.

It was stormy that day, so overcast that I couldn't see the bayou from my room.

He picked a room at random. *Did I stay here?* It didn't seem familiar, nor did the next one, although fleeting wisps of recollection teased his mind. *I might have seen that chair before. Did I sleep in this bed?*

He clearly recalled the next room.

The dumbwaiter stops here. Over there in the corner.

This was Joe's room. Joe somebody. He stayed in this room. But something happened to him. What? I think he got hurt.

Next to the stairway he found a fourth bedroom. He glanced inside, recalled nothing, and walked up the stairs to find open bedrooms on one side of the hall and locked doors on the other.

Craig wouldn't let us go in those rooms. They're the family quarters.

But I went in one. I remember some kind of operating room — or a laboratory. I told Cate about it, so I must have seen it. Think, dammit!

As he looked into the rooms, he recalled that one had been Craig's childhood bedroom. That's where Craig slept that night. Up here on the third floor, away from the rest of us. Me, Marty, Joe and...Alain. Alain Dupont! Lives in Lake Charles. Works for his family's beer distributorship.

Good job, Landry!

He tried the knobs on the locked doors, just in case, but he got nowhere, so he went downstairs to get started. He positioned the video camera toward the corner of the office where the dumbwaiter was. Then he opened the panel and peered into the cramped cubicle, hoping to fill in more of the blanks in his mind. He remembered being inside, but where did it go? To a bedroom and then to the laboratory. Was that right? That part was still tucked away in a corner of his mind, in a place he couldn't yet access.

He knew it would be dark once he started up, so he used his phone as a flashlight and stepped inside the little car. He remembered the dumbwaiter wouldn't start until he closed the panel, which he did. He pressed the button and the tiny elevator began to rise. The quiet clicking of the gears was a familiar sound. Even this early, it seemed coming back to Amelia House was a good way to pull things from the shadows to the forefront of his memory.

The car stopped. He opened the panel and walked into Joe's room. Joe Cochran, who lived in Metairie and was a car salesman. Joe, who hit his head and wasn't feeling well.

This is good. Keep it up!

He stepped back into the little car, slid the panel shut, and pressed the up button. At that moment a huge flash of remembering happened. It was the dumbwaiter. That was how he got into the locked room. That was how he found that strange laboratory.

Someone else had been in the room besides him. Something bad happened there.

Or am I imagining that?

The car rose and then stopped with a slight jerk. He tried to slide the panel, but nothing happened. The dumbwaiter was stuck between floors. He pushed again, harder this time — desperate to open it — but the panel wouldn't budge. He was trapped in a box so small he could barely move.

He had a Swiss Army knife in his pocket, but getting to it would be a challenge. One hand was in front of his body, but the other hung uselessly at his side. He slid the free hand down and slipped it into his pocket while pushing his entire body toward the opposite wall of the car. He brought out the knife, struggled to open it one-handed, and used his teeth to pull out the screwdriver. He tried to pry the panel, but it remained solidly locked in place.

Landry needed air in the cramped sweatbox. He pressed the down button, then the up, but nothing happened. The car didn't move.

Gasping for every breath, he pressed them over and over, frantically jamming his finger into the buttons and shouting, "Move, dammit!" Sweat poured down his face, and panic swept over him. He hit the button with his fist and dropped the phone. It fell face-up between his legs, and now the only illumination was the faint glow from his phone screen on the floor.

Calm down and stay focused. He must have repeated those words a hundred times as he forced himself to take slow, deep breaths and think of a way to get his phone back into his hands. He couldn't reach down, but he thought he might use one shoe to tilt it on its side and move it gingerly up his leg. If he could get it to his crotch, he could reach it.

It took several tries and a lot of shifting around before he found a way to jam one leg into a corner and get sufficient clearance to raise his knee. Raising the phone to his thigh, he dropped it once, then again, and then a third time.

Landry took a break to relax his nerves and noticed a tiny sliver of light where the floor met a side panel. Placing his forehead against the door, he looked down and saw why the car had stopped.

Light filtered in from below, and that meant a panel was open, and they must be closed for the dumbwaiter to work. It had operated fine a few minutes ago, and he'd opened and shut the second-floor panel. Now one of them was open, and that meant only one thing.

Someone had come in the house, a person who knew about the hidden elevator and how to access it. Someone who understood that if they opened a panel, they could trap him.

He'd been uneasy and a little frantic, but now things were magnified a thousandfold. Not only was he locked in a tight box inside the walls, it was no accident that he was here. Whoever had opened that panel knew exactly what would happen. Landry was locked inside a wooden coffin.

Bile rose in his throat. His skin was clammy, and he began to feel light-headed. He tried to kick at the panel but couldn't get his foot back far enough for a decent swing. He beat on it with his fist and pushed with one knee, but nothing worked. Picking up his phone to call for help was his only hope.

Again he slowly moved the phone up one leg with the other foot. If he could get it just two inches above his kneecap, he'd be good. He scrunched down as if trying to sit, allowing his hand to extend a bit further. Each time the phone fell, he tried again, because he was out of ideas.

More than two hours passed. He dozed off a couple of times, and he needed to use the bathroom, but he kept trying. He focused every fiber of his body and mind on the phone, and he slowly moved it up and up, higher and higher, until his bent leg throbbed in pain. Ignoring the discomfort, he forced it even higher, up to his knee. He carefully extended his arm until his fingertips touched the case. One more inch. Just one more inch of bending down or pushing up would do it.

Flashes of pain shot through the sciatic nerve in his hip and leg as he contorted his body even more. He wondered if he might dislocate something, but it didn't matter. He was almost there. Gritting his teeth and crying out in agony, he pushed his leg up and grasped the phone case between his index and middle fingers.

Now it was a battle to hang on. His leg was going numb and his fingers weren't far behind. He inched the phone up a millimeter at a time, and at last he wrapped his fingers around it.

THE EXPERIMENTS: THE BAYOU HAUNTING 5

The phone was in his hand, but when he moved his leg back to the floor, it wouldn't support his weight, and he ended up hunched over and wedged tight in the dumbwaiter. It didn't matter. Until help arrived, he could endure anything. He hit the button and turned on the phone to call 911.

No service.

From this place deep inside the walls of the old house, his phone couldn't pick up a signal. He laughed and cried as he pressed the send button a thousand times. He giggled uncontrollably as he read the same message over and over.

No service.

"You win," he shouted to whoever had opened that panel and trapped him here. "You win. I'm going to die."

With every muscle and sinew screaming for relief, he passed out from panic and sheer exhaustion.

CHAPTER TWENTY-FOUR

"Landry, where are you? Are you in there? Can you hear me?"

In his dream, someone called his name from far, far away. The voice was faint, but out there somewhere, a person was looking for him. He tried to answer, but he was entombed alive in a wooden casket, and no one could hear his plea for help. He called out again.

"I'm buried here in the ground! Help me. Someone, help me, please!"

"Landry, answer me! Where are you?"

I'm…wherever this is. I don't know where I am.

His eyes popped open. He pulled the phone from his shirt pocket — it was almost six p.m., and he'd been in here for hours.

"Landry!" That voice again! Not in a dream this time, but the faint sound of someone calling his name.

He banged on the front panel of the dumbwaiter and screamed for help.

This time the voice resounded from the shaft below him.

"Landry! Are you up there?" He exhaled with relief. Thank God she had come.

"Cate! Cate! Yes, above you. I'm trapped in the dumbwaiter!"

"Oh my God. What do I do?"

"Close the panel. Just slide it shut and let me try the controls." In case they didn't work, he told her how to open the panel again. At least they could talk, even if he couldn't escape.

He pressed the down button and the gears began to whirr softly. The car passed the second floor and stopped at the bottom. He slid the panel open, and she cried out when she saw his contorted body. He told her which of his limbs to extricate first, and he winced in pain as she freed him. As he fell to the floor, he proclaimed that stretching his body was the finest thing he'd ever felt and asked her to help him stand up.

The bathroom was first for him, with water a close second. She helped him hobble to the toilet and got him a bottle of water, and they sat on a couch in the office.

"You're all sweaty and you looked like a sardine in a can! What happened to you?"

"I was in there for hours. Thank God you came, but what are you doing here? Why did you leave me in there so long?"

"What are you talking about?"

"Why did you wait so long to open the panel? And for that matter, how'd you know it was there in the first place?"

"I don't know what you're talking about. I arrived ten minutes ago. The door wasn't locked, I found all your gear in here, and I saw the shaft in the corner with the panel open. I started yelling for you, and at last you answered me."

"So you weren't here earlier?"

THE EXPERIMENTS: THE BAYOU HAUNTING 5

"Nope. What would you have done in there if I hadn't shown up?"

He shrugged, admitting he had run out of ideas. "There are three panels, one on each floor. They all have to be closed or the dumbwaiter won't operate. I was inside when someone opened this one. You can see how cramped the compartment is. The caretaker's due back in the morning, and I would have been trapped until then." He paused. "And what the hell are you doing here?"

"Checking on you. I knew where you were going, so I drove to Jeanerette and saw your Jeep parked outside."

"How did you find the house?"

"You called it Amelia House when you talked to Craig. I knew it was in Jeanerette because you spent the weekend here, and I asked a woman on the street for directions."

"Dr. Wallace called you after I left Villemont, didn't she?"

"She's worried about you. She said you discharged yourself, and she assumed you would come here to rebuild the rest of your memory, even though she told you it wasn't a good idea."

He said, "So let me understand. You brought my Jeep back and parked it in the garage. Then you flew back to Galveston two days ago, and then Dr. Wallace called, and then you flew back?"

She smiled and shook her head. "I never went home. After our lunch at Irene's, you told me you wanted to be alone. You needed time to reflect because you were planning how to come here. I understood that after your call with Craig. You may not have realized it, but you needed help. I took your Jeep back to the garage and got a room at the Monteleone. After Dr. Wallace's call, it was clear to me what I had to do. I stayed another night, and I avoided places where I might run into you, which was easy because you're such a creature of habit. Same restaurants, same bars, same everything."

Hearing that fact made him laugh.

"This morning I walked over to the parking garage and saw you'd taken the Jeep, so I rented a car and waited until this afternoon to come here. I wanted to give you plenty of time to get into trouble. Looks like it worked."

He looked at all his equipment. With one exception, the gear was as he had left it. The tripod holding the video camera lay on the floor. The red recording light still glowed brightly.

"Cross your fingers," he exclaimed. "If I'm lucky, I may have video of the person who trapped me in the dumbwaiter."

The camera was motion-activated and hadn't shot much footage. He rewound the tape to the halfway point and viewed what was there. The camera was on the floor, recording a wall across the room, so he went back to the beginning, where he saw himself open the panel, enter the dumbwaiter, and close it behind him. The video paused when the motion stopped and restarted when someone else entered the room.

In one corner of the video footage someone walked into view and looked at Landry's equipment. Landry said, "That's Gerald, the caretaker who let me in. He wasn't supposed to be back until tomorrow." The man walked to the panel in the corner and pushed the button in the bookshelf. When it slid open, he looked up into the shaft.

They watched Gerald walk away from the open panel and over to the camera. He raised his hand until it covered the lens and knocked the camera over. Now the video displayed a wall and they heard Gerald walking around. In seconds the recording stopped.

Cate said, "He trapped you, Landry. I think you should call Craig."

"There's no need to call Mr. Morisset. I can explain everything." They whirled around and confronted Gerald Oubre, who stood in the hallway behind them.

"I'm sorry I knocked over the camera. One of us always stops by in the late afternoon to make sure everything's locked up, and I came out of habit. There sat your Jeep, reminding me I'm supposed to come back tomorrow, not today. I should have gone then, but curiosity got the best of me. I know who you are. Everybody around here does. I shouldn't have come in, but I wondered what kind of investigating you were doing here. I called your name from the hallway, but you didn't answer. I looked at your cameras and stuff, and I saw you had set up the video camera so it would film the wall that the dumbwaiter's in."

"You knew it was there?"

He grinned and said, "You can't keep secrets from housekeepers and caretakers. We know everything because we poke around everywhere!"

"Really? I don't think so. It's almost impossible to find the dumbwaiter. No one told you it was there, but you were not only able to find it, you figured out how to open the panel. I don't believe you."

Cate put her hand on his arm and squeezed it. "Landry, it makes perfect sense. The man has worked everywhere inside this house. I understand what he's saying."

"Well, I guess I'd better leave you two alone. Speaking of which, I didn't know the lady was coming too. That's fine, though. Welcome to Amelia House. Gerald's my name, and if there's anything you all need, Landry's got my number." He grinned and walked out of the room. They waited in silence until they heard the door close.

Night was coming soon, and the corners of the rooms filled with shadows. Cate turned on every light in the office. She asked, "Did that man make you nervous?"

Landry nodded.

"Me too, so explain something to me. He creeped you out, but yet you got aggressive with him. You accused him of lying about the dumbwaiter. We're all alone in this old house, and you confront somebody who might be the Boston Strangler for all you know."

"Maybe I went too far, but I don't believe his story. If it makes you feel better, I'll ask Craig about him."

She said that was a good idea, and he called Craig. His answering service responded, and an operator said she would relay a message to return the call.

"I have to get inside the laboratory, and there's only one way to do it. I'll go all the way up in the dumbwaiter this time, and if anything goes wrong, you're here to help."

She grabbed his arm. "You're going to ride in that thing again? Are you crazy?"

He nodded. "I have to. It sends chills down my spine, but it's the only way to get inside. I have no choice."

"God, Landry, you just pile trouble on yourself and on me too. I'm damned sure not staying down here alone while you ride up through the walls. Take me upstairs and show me where the laboratory is. I'll wait outside the door until you let me in."

"What if I get stuck?"

"You'll have to bang on the walls or something. I'm scared to death of this place. Just get this over fast so we can get out of here."

He took her to the third floor and showed her where to wait. They returned to the office and she waited while he turned on the video camera, opened the panel, got into the box, and slid it shut. When she heard the soft sound of the gears, she ran upstairs and set her phone timer for five minutes. She brought up his number and put her finger next to the call button, even though she knew he wouldn't have a signal inside the wall. She flinched and jumped with every little creak and noise the old house made, and once she thought she saw something move in the shadows behind her.

After what seemed like an eternity, she heard Landry moving around inside the room. The door swung open and she stepped inside. The room was dark, and Landry fumbled for the light switch. His phone rang just as he flipped it on.

"Craig, thanks for calling me back. I have a question for you." As they talked, Cate looked around the room and uttered a horrific shriek, clawing at Landry's sleeve. She gasped for breath and uttered unintelligible syllables as she pointed to the operating table. Then she fainted.

CHAPTER TWENTY-FIVE

"Who's screaming?" Craig said. "Are you in the house? Is someone there with you?"

Landry dropped his phone and knelt beside Cate. He shook her several times until her eyes opened. She stared at him and thrust herself into his arms, sobbing.

"Let's get out of here," she gurgled. "Something terrible is happening in this house. Help me up. Go, Landry. Go now."

He got her on her feet and remembered Craig, who was still on the phone, shouting now. He switched the phone to speaker.

"That's Cate, my girlfriend. Craig, something awful has happened. I'm in the laboratory. There's a man strapped to the table with some kind of ice pick sticking out of his eye!"

"Listen to me! Get out of there now! You don't know what you're into. Get out while you can!"

Landry ran to the door and tugged on it. A moment ago there had been a skeleton key in the lock. That was how he had opened the door. Now not only was the door locked, the key was also gone. He felt in his pockets and looked on the floor.

"Cate! Cate, do you see a key?" She shook her head.

Craig shouted, "Break a window if you have to! Behind the heavy curtains on the far wall. Break a window and jump down to the porch roof below. For God's sake, get out of that room!"

"Call Gerald," Cate stammered. "He can come back and let us out!"

"Gerald?" Craig screamed. "Who's she talking about?"

"The caretaker. Gerald something. He was in the house a few minutes ago. Maybe he's still around."

"Damn right he is. Landry, you're both in grave danger. You must get away from the house."

"What about the man on the table? He's alive…"

"Leave him! You can't help him now. You interrupted them…"

Losing it, Cate clawed at the door. "Open the door," she moaned. "Open the door and get me out of here."

"Who are you talking about that I interrupted? There's nobody else here."

The door flew open and Cate shouted for joy as Gerald walked into the room. "Thank God you came back!" she yelled. "We were locked in here with that…that man. Get me out of here."

He closed the door, pocketed the key and said, "Not quite yet. They'll be thrilled you're here."

The phone was still on speaker mode and Craig shouted, "Jerry, leave them alone. This isn't about them."

Gerald came near the phone. "Craig, is that you? How nice to hear your voice."

"Let them go."

Landry said, "Who are you?" With a smirk, the man grabbed the phone.

"You're the caretaker. You told us that," Cate answered for him, as if saying the words would make them true.

THE EXPERIMENTS: THE BAYOU HAUNTING 5

Gerald pointed to the table and said, "No, my dear. *That's* the caretaker. Craig can tell you who I am."

"I told you to get out," Craig said. "Gerald — Jerry — is my brother."

"Tell them the rest," Gerald said with a smirk.

"He died in the same fire that killed my parents."

"And..."

Silence.

Gerald said, "Ah, my brother seems to forget the most important part of the story. Perhaps his powers of recollection will improve after we conduct experiments on the two of you."

Craig shouted, "No, Jerry! This has nothing to do with them. If I knew what would happen, I would never have done what I did."

"Ah yes, hindsight. If my brother had only known that through some quirk of fate, we were all inextricably linked to this house forever, he would have had second thoughts. Too late, brother. It's time for me to go. We must do things with our new friends." He disconnected the call.

CHAPTER TWENTY-SIX

Keep him talking.

That was all Landry could think to do. Stretch out the time and maybe they could find a way out of this. Cate cowered in a corner, hiding her face with her hands, but Landry stood between Gerald — Jerry now — and the metal table.

"Craig told me over and over that he didn't have a brother."

"That's what he told everybody, even before the fire. He found that way easier. No brother, no explaining. Otherwise people might wonder what was going on inside Amelia House."

"But…but Craig just said you died in the fire. What did he mean by that?"

"Those words so bitter for him to spew, and such sweet music to my ears. Who'd have suspected the genius, the millionaire, the smart one, the…the one so different from his bastard brother. Yes, I died along with Mother and Father."

"You're older than Craig."

"By fifteen years. They forced me to participate in the experiments, at least at first. I began to enjoy helping after I got the orbitoclast."

"The orbitoclast?"

"I see you don't understand. My apologies. Let me show you the tools of our trade." He stepped around Landry, who realized he'd asked something that he shouldn't have.

Jerry pointed to the face of the man who lay strapped to the table, and touched the ice pick that was embedded in his eye socket.

"See that instrument?"

Landry gulped. "Yes. What is it?"

"It's an orbitoclast. Can you imagine what it's for?"

Cate ran to Landry's side and screamed, "Stop it! That's enough. Don't tell me what you've done to this poor man."

Jerry's words were smooth. He was having a great time, and as hard as it would be for Cate, Landry had to keep him talking. It might be the only way to survive.

"This 'poor man,' as you call him, will be fine. No harm done, except a minor alteration here and there. It's like taking your car in for a tune-up. That tool — it's what leukotomists use."

"Leukotomists?"

"People who perform leukotomies. People like these two."

He walked to a corner of the room where an old-fashioned portable privacy screen stood. Landry had seen similar ones in movies — in the old days, they had separated the beds in hospital wards.

Jerry pulled the screen back and revealed two armchairs sitting side by side. Even in partial shadow, he saw the horror of what Jerry revealed.

Sitting in the chairs were two shrunken, shriveled corpses. The flesh on their faces had peeled away, leaving

THE EXPERIMENTS: THE BAYOU HAUNTING 5

skull-like shapes of black. Shreds of clothing stuck to their dried, charred skin. They must have experienced unimaginable agony.

"These are my mother and stepfather, Maria Oubre and Frank Morisset. Say hello, parents."

As Landry stared in shock, he felt something filmy and invisible play lightly across his face. There came a light breeze and then he heard the moans — the same whispering sounds he'd heard just before something unearthly enveloped him and started squeezing and squeezing. It had happened before, on that night when he came to this room during the storm. He remembered. He remembered everything, and he realized he and Cate faced terrible danger.

The horror was returning. Knowing what to expect this time, he fought, flailing his arms against the delicate, invisible cobwebs that swirled around his body. He shouted for Cate to run, to get away from the madness before the cocoon enveloped her too.

The last thing he saw was Cate creeping toward the back of the room while Jerry watched with glee as the vines entwined themselves around Landry. Jerry's thoughts were on him, and Landry prayed Cate would escape.

CHAPTER TWENTY-SEVEN

The moment Jerry hung up, Craig called his pilot, saying he had an emergency and had to get to New Iberia as soon as possible. Craig was in luck, because his pilot had already placed an order for a double bourbon and water. If he'd gotten started, he couldn't have flown for eight hours.

The pilot's friends around the bar of the Caribbean Club in Key Largo chided him for choosing his rich boss over an evening of barroom banter. For a private pilot, it could happen anytime, but it disappointed him nonetheless. Craig rarely called him at the last minute, and he had been looking forward to a few hours with the guys. He told them the boss paid the bills, so he called the shots. As he walked out, he punched the arm of the Humphrey Bogart statue by the door, a piece of memorabilia from the days when scenes from the movie *Key Largo* were shot in this eccentric bar.

Apprehensive, Craig fidgeted in his seat as the jet screamed across the Gulf of Mexico. It wouldn't take long, but every minute counted now.

The plane landed and taxied to the FBO. When his pilot shut down the engines, Craig lowered the stairs himself, ran to the parking lot, and waved at the Uber driver he'd arranged from the plane. "There's a hundred bucks tip for you if you get me to Jeanerette in under ten minutes," he said, and the driver nodded, knowing that was easy money because at this time of night the highway was deserted. Uber didn't like drivers who exceeded the speed limit, but this driver was already deciding what he'd buy with his fat tip.

When they arrived at Amelia House, Craig tossed the money into the front seat and jumped out. A girl sat on the back porch stoop. Clearly in shock, she looked up at him through unseeing eyes.

"Are you Cate?"

"I rode the dumbwaiter down," she mumbled. "Landry's locked in that room with him. Please help him. Please." She rose and followed him into the house.

They bounded up the stairs and Craig used his key to open the laboratory door, and Cate pointed at the operating table. Craig wasn't sure what he'd find in the room, but when he surveyed the horrific scene, it was almost too much to comprehend.

The disfigured, burned cadavers of Frank and Maria Morisset stood on the far side of the operating table. There came an unearthly cackle from Craig's mother when she saw him. She raised her fleshless arm and pointed a bony finger.

Jerry was on the side closest to them, and there was an unconscious man strapped to the table. He was covered to his neck in sheets, and the bright surgical lamp illuminated his face. Craig half-expected it would be Landry, but he had never seen this person. Jerry glanced at Craig and said, "Well, the gang's all here. I couldn't have hoped for more. We're about to operate. Want to be our assistant? It'll be like old times."

"You're...you're alive," Craig exclaimed. "You can't be."

"Come on, little brother. Of all people, you know I'm not alive. And I can't explain it. Can you, Father?" With a laugh, he gestured toward one of the black things across from him.

Cate grabbed Craig's arm and pointed across the room. "Please help Landry!"

A six-foot cocoon stood near the cloth-covered windows. He could see tendrils moving, weaving, dancing as they whirled around and around. There was no question what it meant, because he'd been enveloped too when he was last here. The corpses somehow conjured the vines.

"Leave him alone!" Jerry ordered. "He's next, unless you'd like to cut in line!"

Craig saw his brother insert the pick-like instrument — the orbitoclast — guiding it around the man's eyeball and through the socket. He understood what was happening; as a child he'd served as assistant during the procedures.

"Who is he?"

"He's the maintenance man. When these two arrived, I convinced them I was him."

"You're dead. Why are you still doing this?"

"I'm only dead thanks to you," Jerry smirked. "You never embraced what Mother and Father were doing. You never tried to learn. It was fascinating to me, and thanks to them, I turned out like this instead of being shriveled corpses like they are."

A malevolent wail issued forth from one of the figures across the table. It was a bone-jarring sound that shook the room.

"Shut up, Mother. Be happy my lobotomy worked. One of us is normal, even in death."

Craig said, "What do you mean, your lobotomy worked?"

"Father altered my brain. Don't ask me how. Don't ask *them* how either, because no one knows for sure. I can appear to you as a flesh-and-blood person although I've been dead for seventeen years, and all because Father tweaked something special in my brain!"

"That doesn't explain why they burned in the flames and you didn't."

"Mother and Father look like that because the chemicals exploded right in front of them. They burned to a crisp, but I didn't die that way. I was in another room. I suffocated from inhaling the smoke. You should try it yourself — it's an interesting way to die. But I have other plans for your demise, because you're the only Morisset left. When I kill you tonight, then I can live forever."

Craig ran to Landry, and Jerry screamed with crazed glee. "Don't get too close, brother! You know what will happen. Those wispy little curls will capture you too!"

Craig had a desperate idea he hoped would work. He tugged at the black cloth covering the window until it tore and fell to the floor. Moonlight shone through the tall, grimy windows. He grabbed a chair and threw it through the window with a tremendous crash. The work at the operating table stopped as if he'd hit a pause button, and he reached through the viselike rings, grabbed Landry, heaved him up, and tossed him out the window.

Cate screamed as a ghastly howl came from the table and the room began spinning crazily. She and Craig watched figures fly through the air — ethereal bodies, all corpses of the Morisset men and women who had performed the fiendish experiments in this room.

The fiendish frenzy only lasted a few seconds. The figures disappeared, and all that remained was a body on the table, Cate standing by the doorway, and Landry's cry for help coming through the broken window.

She ran over, brushed away shards of glass, and looked out. He lay just four feet below, on the roof of the second-floor veranda. His leg was twisted to one side, and when she called to him, he said he thought he'd broken it.

THE EXPERIMENTS: THE BAYOU HAUNTING 5

"I'll get help. Just stay there!" She shouted for Craig to come assist Landry. She searched the room and realized when everything else disappeared, so had he.

CHAPTER TWENTY-EIGHT

"Help me! Help me, please!" A whimper came from the lips of the unfortunate man strapped to the table. Cate ran to his side and looked into his face.

"You must lie still," she said, but he begged for her to release him. She had to assist Landry, but this man needed her help too. She pulled away the sheets and loosened the straps that restrained his arms and legs. He sat up and stretched.

He wanted to talk, and although she had other priorities, she listened because of the trauma he'd endured. Landry needed her help, but for a few minutes he'd be okay where he lay.

The man said, "First there were these vines. They wrapped around me and trapped me somehow. Some people moved me around and strapped me to this table. A man stood over me holding two little metal rods that he put to my temples. Once that happened, everything went blank." Cate looked at his eye; the skin around the socket was turning purple from whatever they did to him. The metal pick that Jerry brandished now lay on the table.

"How do you feel?" she asked, and he said it was like being run over by an eighteen-wheeler. "The problem's in my head. Man, it's throbbing like crazy. Worst headache I ever had." He gripped the table to steady himself, stood and took a few hesitant steps.

He looked around the room. "The window's broken. What happened?"

"My boyfriend fell to the roof below. Are you steady enough to help me rescue him?"

The man — Gabby, he said his name was — looked out the window and told Craig help was on the way. "I'm a little shaky," he admitted, "but together we can get him off the roof."

He took her to a shed adjoining the house that held a variety of tools and equipment. With some effort they carried a ten-foot ladder and a stout coil of rope to the laboratory, maneuvered the ladder through the window, and she crawled down to where Landry lay.

He winced when Cate touched his left thigh. He tried to stand, but his leg wobbled, and he fell. Cate dialed 911 and stayed on the roof with him while Gabby went to the back porch to wait for an ambulance.

She explained to Landry that Craig had showed up and witnessed the bizarre things happening around the operating table. He'd picked up the cocoon that enveloped Landry and threw it out the window.

"That probably saved my life," he said.

"Things got even crazier after that. You can't imagine how bizarre things got. The room flew into a frenzy. I saw ghostlike things, those black corpses and Jerry — who's dead too, but you wouldn't know it — and Craig. Then all of them disappeared. We have to find Craig, but we have to take care of you first. I'm calling the police."

He took her hand and said, "Let's don't do that yet. I'm starting to understand what all of this means, and getting the cops involved won't help. It would only complicate things for me, and they'll never believe what happened anyway. I have to let this play out."

"I'll have to trust you on that one. But what do we do next? We can't leave with Craig still in the house somewhere. He could be in danger."

"If my hunch is correct, he's not in danger, at least for now. He knows a lot more than we do about all this. Let's get me to a doctor, and then we'll come back for Craig."

"So you believe he's still in the house?"

"I'm positive he is. The family wields some kind of power over this place — you saw it today, and I experienced it last time too. Today even though I was engulfed in those tendrils, I could hear everything that was going on. He may not be evil like the others, but the Morisset blood runs in his veins too. I'm beginning to think he has secrets we can't imagine."

After an hour and a fire engine's cherry picker, the rescuers strapped Landry to a stretcher, lowered him to the ground, and loaded him in an ambulance for a ride to the hospital.

"Do we need to call the police?" a medical tech asked before they left, and Landry assured them everything was fine. "I had an accident. I fell out the window, simple as that." His story didn't sound that simple to the EMTs, but they didn't press things. Their job was to care for patients, not to interrogate them.

CHAPTER TWENTY-NINE

There was good news. Landry's lower leg was badly bruised but not broken. They left the hospital around four a.m., and he sported a knee-high boot. As Cate drove him back to Jeanerette, he remarked again on how accurately he now remembered that lost reunion weekend. As awful as it had been, going back to the house had accomplished what he hoped. He recalled everything.

Back at Amelia House they found Gabby sitting in his truck, where he said he'd been since they left. "I'm not going back inside. I know who you are, Mr. Drake, because I recognized you. When I thought about what happened to me, it made perfect sense why you're here. Supernatural stuff's going on and you're investigating it." He didn't give Landry a chance to answer. Gabby had a lot to get off his chest, and he'd been waiting all this time for them to return.

"After the Morissets died in that fire, their rich kid Craig never came back. No funeral, nothing. That's when the stories started about the house being haunted. People said because they didn't get proper funerals, their burned corpses roamed the halls of Amelia House at night. I've been a caretaker here nine years, and not once have I ever set foot inside that house after dark. I'm not afraid of much, but ghosts and the undead — those are something a man needs to be wary of. That's what those people are, right? Ghosts? That's what it looks like to me."

"Me too," Landry replied. That was enough information for now. Jerry called them his parents, but since Gabby was unconscious, he didn't hear it. The man had suffered an ordeal, been the subject of a bizarre operation, and he had been shaken to his very core. What purpose would be served to tell Gabby that three dead Morissets stood around that operating table? He already had suffered enough horror to last a lifetime.

As before, talking seemed to be Gabby's catharsis. "The more I recalled about what happened to me, the more spooked I got. I'll never go back. Look at my eye. Looks like I went ten rounds with Muhammad Ali. What do you figure they wanted by operating on me?"

Landry shrugged, although he understood what they had been up to. It was something else to tell him later, not now.

"We shouldn't go back alone either," Cate said, but Landry had other ideas.

"This is what I do. If I ran away from every unexplained thing that happened, I wouldn't have any *Bayou Hauntings* shows. I just regret that I don't have footage of the laboratory, but maybe Craig will let me recreate it later."

To Gabby he said, "Craig Morisset's in there somewhere. We saw him in the laboratory while you lay on the table, but he disappeared. He came here to help us, and now I have to go find him. You're free to go. You're not a part of this, and I don't blame you a bit for leaving after what you've been through."

"I kinda feel like I'm deserting you two."

THE EXPERIMENTS: THE BAYOU HAUNTING 5

"Go," Cate said, trying to sound more confident than she felt. "Check on us in a few hours, and let's see how things are going then."

As Gabby drove away down the lane, Landry said, "I'm proud of you, but you don't have to go with me. Why don't you wait in the Jeep and let me look around?"

"The way I see it, the only thing more insane than my going back in there is letting you do it alone. I've come this far and you're not getting rid of me now."

"It could be dangerous…"

"Knock it off, okay? Craig threw you out the window to keep his family of ghouls from killing you. Yeah, it could be dangerous. In fact, the more I talk, the more terrified I'm getting. If we're going in, let's get it over with."

Streaks of pink crept up the eastern sky. Dawn was coming soon, a time when everything that the night made frightening seems less spooky and more explainable. He thought about waiting until the sun rose — perhaps driving over to Coach's diner for coffee and donuts — but hours had passed since Craig disappeared in the laboratory. Landry wanted to help him, even though he doubted Craig faced danger from his own family. There was a reason why they clung to this side of the spiritual realm, and Landry was certain everything tied back to Craig. They wanted something only he could provide.

They entered the house and went directly to the laboratory to try the door. Although he knew it would be locked, he'd hoped for a break this time, and they were relieved to see the door standing open. A predawn glow filtered through the broken window, bathing the shadowy room and the metal table with an eerie phosphorescence. When he flipped the switch, the surgical lamp illuminated the center of the room.

There was no sign of the earlier chaos. The operating table was empty, and its sheets were neatly arranged. No corpses sat in chairs behind a screen, and no person living or dead was in the room except for the two of them. The medical tools were back on their metal tray, all arranged in tidy rows, and the glass on the floor by the window gave the only sign that what they experienced really happened.

The table stood as a reminder that the Morissets performed horrific procedures here, but a casual visitor to Amelia House might not think it unusual to discover a laboratory in the ancestral home of a family that included two self-made physicians.

"I'll try Craig's cell phone," Landry said. "If he's in the house, maybe we can hear it." He looked at the screen. "Holy crap!"

"What?"

"I missed a text from Craig when we were at the hospital." He read it aloud.

Whatever you do, stay away from the house. Don't go inside! You'll never escape this time. Call me when you finish at the hospital, and I'll meet you to explain everything.

"Now there's a warning you should have listened to," a voice said from somewhere out in the hall. Smooth and even but filled with hatred and menace, they knew that voice well by now.

CHAPTER THIRTY

"Run, Cate!"

Cate raced down the stairway to the ground floor, with Landry hobbling behind her as fast as his lame leg would allow. As they neared the door, they found Jerry standing with arms out wide, blocking it. His face was contorted into a clownish smirk and he roared, "You mustn't leave so soon! Why, you've only just arrived. We have plans for you, so I must insist you stay. There are experiments we want to perform, but with my brother's help, you escaped. Now that he's gone, we can continue."

Cate cried, "He's dead! He's like an apparition. We can run through him and get out!"

They sprang forward and Jerry cackled, "You might get past me, but I'm afraid those pesky things are a different story!" He pointed to the floor, where much larger tendrils than they'd seen earlier slithered across the hallway. The vines reached their ankles, wrapped around them, and jerked Landry and Cate to the ground.

Landry saw that the coils emanated from a doorway to the right where the corpses stood in the half-light.

"We have to get out fast!" he shouted to Cate. He reached for a tendril crawling up her pant leg, but it reacted like a snake — twisting, turning and staying out of his reach, anticipating his moves. He took out the Swiss Army knife, snapped open the largest blade, and sliced cleanly through one of the wriggling coils.

Dark red blood spurted from the cut, startling them. Landry cried out in alarm and drew back.

"Didn't expect them to bleed, did you?" Jerry snarled, his face a mask of evil. "They're as real as you are!"

As Landry hacked away, blood spattered his clothes and pooled on the floor. Little by little, he made progress. At least he'd figured out how to stop them, but it might already be too late. Instead of cutting at the ends, he scooted down the hallway and cut a vine in the middle. When he did, the end entwined around his legs released its hold and withered. The problem was how to cut fast enough. The vines were no thicker than a spear of asparagus, but there were dozens of them now.

He made headway, and when only a few vines remained, he moved to help Cate. Wrapped to her knees, she cried in pain as he began to cut and they tightened their grip. His plan was working, but there were too many. He'd never cut them all in time.

"Cate, don't give up. I have an idea."

He sliced away enough vines from his feet to stand and limped to the doorway where the zombielike carcasses stood. Not knowing if it would work, he thrust his foot with a karate kick into the torso of the nearest corpse. Instead of connecting with flesh and bone, it kept moving as if he'd struck a cloud.

The scream that issued forth from Jerry's lips was the most unearthly, horrifying sound imaginable. It was deep and from somewhere far away — a place in the realm of the dead. The corpse disintegrated into a million motes of black dust that swirled into the air.

THE EXPERIMENTS: THE BAYOU HAUNTING 5

"That worked!" Cate yelled, but then Jerry took a step toward her.

"You can't hurt me," she screamed at him. "I'm not afraid of you!"

Landry glanced at the floor. Cate was right. When the corpse exploded, half the vines disappeared along with it. He backed away to kick at the other figure, but both it and Jerry vanished. And so did the remaining tendrils.

Landry helped Cate stand.

"What...what happened?"

Landry couldn't tell her. "I've never experienced something like this. You and I faced anguished spirits in the nursery at Jordan Blanchard's house, and I saw tormented souls in the old asylum at Victory, but this is different. Let's get out of here and call Craig." They jumped in the Jeep and sped away.

When they drove into downtown Jeanerette, Cate expressed the feeling they both had. Minutes ago they were fighting mysterious vines controlled by a pair of corpses, while here — mere blocks away from Amelia House — life was normal. A school bus rumbled down the street. People walked into the post office and the bank. Even the traffic signal was a beacon to the tranquility of Main Street USA. Life went on in this small town while death reigned in a house on the other side of the bayou.

She said, "How about we head back to New Orleans and write this one off to experience? I won't even make you go back to the clinic like you're supposed to. I'll certify your sanity myself."

"If you tell anyone what just happened, you'll get a sanity check too. There's nothing wrong with my mind and you know it. It's my memory, and I think after the last few hours, everything's back. I remember every detail of the nights I spent in New Iberia and the one at Amelia House. But if you're serious, you can leave. You don't have to stay here with me."

"I was just kidding about your sanity, although I do wonder what it'll take to stop you from doing crazy things. And of course I have to stay here with you. Who's left to save your ass if I go?"

He laughed, parked his SUV and called Craig, whose first question was if Landry's leg was okay.

"It's just bruised," he said, "but I need to tell you something. I didn't see your text in time."

"When I didn't hear, I was afraid of that. What happened, and are you all okay?"

Landry gave him a brief recap of their terrifying minutes at Amelia House. "We only got away because I hit one of the corpses," he said. "It disintegrated before our eyes, and then Jerry and the other one disappeared."

As bizarre as that statement was, it didn't seem to surprise Craig, who said if they'd meet him in the cemetery, he would explain everything.

CHAPTER THIRTY-ONE

Only a few blocks from the cemetery, they arrived before Craig. Landry pointed out the imposing structure gleaming in the sunlight as they walked through the aboveground graves.

As they surveyed the marble edifice, Cate asked, "Why are there so many empty spaces? I guess whoever built it wanted plenty of room for family members in years to come."

"Somehow I don't think that's it. I asked Craig the last time I came, and he called it none of my business. He doesn't talk about his family, and now I understand why not. I sensed the animosity last time, but until what just happened, I didn't realize how frighteningly deep all this hatred runs.

"His people were insane and hellish pseudo-physicians who even experimented on their own children. Perhaps Craig's father did discover the secret to life after death — if you call Jerry's situation a life. I don't think Craig's as insane as the family, but he carries the genes. He's far from normal — you haven't seen him withdraw into a state of — I can't describe it. It's not a blackout, but it's not amnesia.

It's as if he knows what he's doing, but he's gone somewhere far away from the real world."

She watched Craig get out of a pickup and walk into the graveyard. Landry asked where he got the ride, and he said he'd paid a guy at a used-car lot a hundred bucks to borrow it for a few days. Craig studied every faceplate, running his fingers over a few inscriptions as though they were unfamiliar.

"I owe you an explanation," he began, but Landry interrupted.

"Before you start, I owe you more than that. You threw me out the window to save my life, didn't you?"

Craig nodded.

Cate said, "You had us worried. I turned around and you'd disappeared. Where did you go?"

"Away. The house is full of secret places, even ones Jerry isn't aware of."

He stared into Landry's eyes with an intensity that forced Landry to look away. "I threw you out the window because they wanted you. The caretaker's surgery was underway. They had you wrapped up and ready to go next."

Cate wondered how the other caretakers worked in the house. Didn't they get captured too? Craig explained that until the other day when he opened the closet, they'd been in a state of dormancy he didn't understand.

Cate said, "Have you seen the vines? They're terrifying."

"Yes. They create them somehow. The vines incapacitate their subjects so they can administer an electroconvulsive shock. That knocks the patient out and the procedure begins."

Now Landry understood what Gabby meant when he said a man had held metal rods to his temples. "What kind of procedure was it?"

"It'll be easier to understand if I start from the beginning. After my parents died, I did everything possible

THE EXPERIMENTS: THE BAYOU HAUNTING 5

to be sure no visitors would ever set foot inside the house. Strange things have always gone on there, and Jerry and my parents rank among the strangest Morissets of all. Even with them dead, I feared that outsiders would be in danger.

"By banning people from the house, I also kept the family's secrets intact. I swore I would never come back because something might happen. I guess after seventeen years I got complacent. I'd come only for the reunion. I wouldn't go to Jeanerette at all. I'd stay in New Iberia and attend the functions there.

"It shocked me when you showed up at the party that night. You were the last person I expected to run into, and seeing you made me nervous as hell. I knew what to expect from you — questions, demands to look around inside the house, and all the stuff investigators do. I refused to let you in because of the risk involved. Same for Marty and the others. I feared if I returned, I couldn't control what they might do.

"The thing that changed my mind was the storm. I'd already been to the house by then. That should have been enough to stop me, but I gave in because we needed shelter for just one night. A single night. What harm would it be? Harm? What was I thinking? Someone might have died that day, and Joe Cochran will never be the same, because they got him. If I hadn't let you in, it would never have happened. Thanks to me, they got their next victim."

"I don't understand."

"Remember the bruises around Joe's eye? And the instrument in the caretaker's eye today?"

"Yeah. I saw one of those when we were at the house with you, displayed on a shelf in the office. Jerry called it an orbitoclast."

"And the operation was a leukotomy. My ancestors used that archaic name to make themselves feel better about it, I suppose. The Nazis called it by a more familiar name, a lobotomy. You go in through the eye socket, penetrate the skull, and manipulate areas of the brain."

Cate said, "How long has this been going on?"

"Far too long. My great-grandfather Marco installed the laboratory when he built the house. The public considered him a wonderful, caring man — a traveling physician who rode the parishes in a horse-drawn carriage to treat the sick. That part's true, but Marco's trade had a dark side. Now and then people would disappear in remote areas of a nearby parish. They'd go fishing or hunting and never come home. Perhaps they hitched a ride with a friendly man who offered to take them to the next town.

"Nobody ever suspected everyone's family doctor, the man who delivered babies, prescribed home remedies for all kinds of problems, and worked for free if they weren't able to pay. Nobody suspected that he drugged men, hauled them back to Amelia House, and tried out theories on their brains."

Craig pointed to the top row of crypts. "Remember the last time you and I came here?" he said to Landry. "You asked why the mausoleum had so many empty spaces. I didn't answer you then, but there are no more secrets now. Almost every crypt has bodies."

Landry didn't understand. "Then why are there no names on most of the faceplates?"

"Think about it and you'll figure it out."

Cate understood before Landry. "The ones buried in those crypts are the people your ancestors operated on. Am I right?"

"Yes. Marco buried his victims in the woods, but his son, Albert, and my parents decided the mausoleum would be a great alternative. They crammed the corpses of unknown men two or three to a crypt and left them to rot."

Landry said, "I wouldn't have thought they'd bury them right next to the family members. It sounds a little…well, ghoulish, to be honest."

THE EXPERIMENTS: THE BAYOU HAUNTING 5

"But the thing to understand is that these men — these self-proclaimed doctors — thought they were on a noble quest. They performed experiments that might unlock the mysteries of the brain. Their pitiable subjects gave their lives for the common good. At least that's what three generations of Morissets told themselves to cover up their serial killings."

"When did you find out about all of this?"

"When I was around four or five years old. Jerry was fifteen years older than I am. My mother was sixteen and unmarried when she had Jerry. She married Frank a few years later, and I came along in 1980. My grandfather Albert brainwashed my father into helping with the experiments, and later my mother became fascinated with them. She held the nefarious title of the first Morisset woman to play an active part.

"My parents believed they would make medical history. They recruited Jerry to help — they had him performing lobotomies and hauling bodies to the cemetery at night before he turned eighteen. When I was a little boy, they made me stand by the table and learn the names of all the instruments. I'd hand them to my mother or father when they asked."

"What were they after?"

"Perfection, I guess. They wanted to tweak various parts of the brain and find out what happened. Would personality change? Or attitude, or physical abilities? The problem was, they couldn't afford to keep their subjects around long enough to study the results. Once the men — and they were all men — woke up, none of them was much interested in sticking around."

"Did people die from the operation?"

"No. It was simple, quick and almost painless. The patient might have a headache, but nothing more. He'd be different, of course. Maybe it would be how he processed things, or created memories, or how quickly he responded to questions. It might be anything, and that's what Marco was looking for. What changes could he create in a human brain by tweaking this part or that, turning the instrument just a millimeter to the right instead of the left, or probing a millimeter deeper than before?

"Back in the early days — in the nineteen twenties and thirties when my great-grandfather Marco was the doctor — he'd keep the patients alive for weeks or months and observe their behavior. He'd put them to work in the house or the cane fields and pay them enough so they'd stay. Most of them didn't even know he'd operated on them because of the anesthesia and electric shock they used. There were stubborn ones, others who were uncooperative and belligerent, and still others who threatened blackmail. A sad few lost all cognitive ability when Dr. Marco botched the operation."

Landry asked what happened to those people.

"He studied them for a while — same for grandfather Albert — but the family had a term for what happened next. Elimination."

"How about the patients your father operated on?"

"I know from experience what happened. In a modern society, they were afraid to imprison their victims, but they couldn't afford for even one to get away. At first they'd keep the poor people bound and gagged for a day or two and then eliminate them. But then it changed, and they started killing their patients immediately after the surgery. There was no pretense of scientific study by that point. I began to realize that they were in this for the thrill of it. It was exciting to play God with a person's brain, and it became murder for the fun of it. Have I mentioned my father and mother were insane?"

"My God," Cate exclaimed. "What a horrific way to grow up. You said you saw what your own parents did, but how do you know about the operations your grandfather and his father performed?"

THE EXPERIMENTS: THE BAYOU HAUNTING 5

"Because they wrote everything down. The building in the woods held records of every surgery performed at Amelia House. It would surprise you how many notes they kept — there were boxes and boxes filled with incredibly detailed notes about the operations. I would sneak in there and read them. That's how I found out the other family secret. I don't know whether it was Marco or Albert who came up with a brilliant idea. They didn't have to rely on recalcitrant subjects whom they were forced to eliminate before studies could be done. They began operating on family members instead."

"How many family members…" Cate asked, almost afraid to hear the answer.

"My guess is all of them. Maybe that's how Marco's little baby died." He pointed to the top row of the mausoleum. "There she lies. Baby Girl Morisset."

Claiming exhaustion, Craig walked to a nearby marble vault and sat down.

Landry said, "Living with this must be pure hell."

"It isn't possible for you to understand half of what I've gone through. The Morissets are a family of monsters. Every one of us. Even the children."

"You can't blame yourself."

He looked in Landry's eyes. "As I said earlier, you couldn't possibly understand."

Cate decided it was time to talk about something else. "Back at the house we saw the…uh, the bodies of your mother and father. Am I saying that right? Is that what those…those things were?"

He nodded. "That's what they still are."

"The mausoleum has spaces with their names on them. Are their…bodies buried there, even though we saw them at the house?"

"No, and that's the one thing I regret about my family. Everyone in town thinks I never came back to Jeanerette after the fire. They blame me for callously abandoning my heritage because I didn't give them a funeral and I locked up Amelia House. I'll let you in on a secret. It's not my deepest, darkest one, but it's something no one else knows.

"Although almost no one knew, I briefly returned to Jeanerette after the fire to take care of some business. I lived in Lafayette then and I was the next of kin. As the only living relative, everything was in my hands. After the medical examiner ruled their deaths accidental, I had the bodies delivered to the house. It would have been blasphemous to have funerals after what these despicable people did. I carried the cadavers to my parents' bedroom and stuffed all three of them into the back of a closet. I locked it and also the doors to the family quarters and the laboratory. From then on, those rooms remained off-limits. Even maintenance people couldn't enter. I installed security cameras in the hallway to make sure nobody disobeyed my order."

He stood and walked back to the mausoleum. "I'm just like them. What's the difference between hiding their bodies in the house and stuffing them into empty crypts?"

"You're too hard on yourself. It's not the same thing," Cate said.

"You're right; it isn't. It's worse. I brought Landry and the others to the house, even though I knew how evil it is. I was naive. You watched my parents. They acquired some kind of power — they can move about like zombies, but their bodies are charred husks. With Jerry, my father finally achieved his medical miracle, but he never knew it. I was the first to observe my father's breakthrough when I opened the closet two weeks ago. Somehow, he stopped a dead body from decaying, allowing it to walk and move and talk almost as if alive. Almost, but not quite.

"Without realizing it, I hid my parents' bodies in a sanctuary — their shrine to bizarre, evil medical experimentation. I put them in a place they loved — where they and theirs had committed mortal sins. Granted, I locked up the house and kept unsuspecting locals out. Then after all those years I delivered new victims to them. You, Landry, and the others."

He extended his hands toward the empty crypts that bore the names of his mother and father, and his eyes glazed over as if he was staring at something far away.

"Watch him," Landry whispered. "He's leaving us — he's going into his other state. This is what I told you about."

Why couldn't you have left us alone? You had subjects to work on. But that wasn't enough, Mother. You thought you were a god with the power to alter the human brain, and you even experimented on those who should have been dearest to you. I understand why my father did it. The Morisset blood ran in his veins. He was just like his ancestors — Hell's surgeons — because he was destined to be a murderer like his own father and grandfather. But not you. You birthed both of us. We were flesh of your flesh, but you used your babies for gruesome experiments. You chose what you did, and that makes you more evil than he ever was.

Cate stepped toward him.

"Don't," Landry cautioned, but she touched Craig's arm.

He jerked back and gave her a hard push. "Leave me!" he screamed, his voice echoing against the mausoleum that bore his family name. "Leave me alone!"

Startled by his reaction, she backed away and told Landry they should leave.

"Wait for me in the car. I've left every other time. I want to watch this all the way through."

CHAPTER THIRTY-TWO

Craig realized Landry was standing nearby and said, "How long was I gone?"

"Fourteen minutes."

"Tell me about it."

"I will, but first I want you to tell me what just happened. How long have you been experiencing the — what are they — trances? What causes them?"

"Since the twenty-fourth day of January 1989. You've seen them, so call them whatever you want. I call them lapses. As to what causes them, it's about things I once had but lost. Things they took away from me, like memories, regret, conscience and morality. Things like that trigger my lapses."

Landry said he didn't understand.

Craig glared at him and said, "And I don't care. I didn't ask you to come here, and you've seen too much. You broke a promise when you brought the girl to the house. The deal was you'd come alone, and now the deal's off."

"Yeah, I agreed to come alone, but I didn't bring her. I sent her home, but she followed me here. Except for Cate I'd still be trapped in the dumbwaiter. Before your lapse, you explained about your parents' bodies. Tell me more about that. Better yet, let's get out of here and go to town or something. Being in this place is hard for you. I understand that."

Landry's sympathetic words fell on deaf ears. The once-broken man who stood before him now was cynical and curt.

"You understand nothing of what I feel. What I told you hardly scratches the surface of the horrors of Amelia House and my family. I'm one of them, not one of your kind. Can you understand *that*?"

Landry said, "You called them Hell's surgeons."

He raised his eyebrows. "And?"

"Is that what they called themselves?"

"Are you kidding? I told you they were after a medical breakthrough. None of them had one iota of remorse for what they did to other human beings."

"And you said your mother allowed your father to experiment on Jerry. And you."

Craig boiled over with anger. He struggled to restrain an intense urge to destroy Landry. That rage swept through him every time he realized that while everyone else was normal, his only claim to normality was a facade he hid behind every day of his life.

"I will not allow you to expose my family. With the resources I have, I can keep you from revealing what you think you've discovered. Don't push me, Landry. I'm not who you think I am. I'm one of them. I'm a Morisset, the son of my father. You can get hurt looking in places that need to stay hidden."

Just then Cate walked up and said, "Craig, are you feeling okay? I thought I'd better come back and check."

"Is your threat aimed at her too, Craig?" Landry said as Cate looked at him in astonishment. "Will you hurt her too, just because she's here with me? I've only known you two weeks, but I don't think you're like them. They did horrible things to you and other people, but you're a decent person. I'm giving you a chance to settle things once and for all. You've lived with lapses since 1989. You even recall the exact day they started. Let me try to help you make a fresh start without lapses and without guilt."

With eyes wide, Craig stared at Landry as though he was a complete idiot.

"*You* help *me*? You can't imagine how deeply I'm involved in this. None of this would have happened if I had stayed away. Now it's too late for both of us."

He paused, gazed off somewhere and listened. Then he spoke.

He's going to reveal some of it anyway. You can't do anything about it, and I refuse to be your puppet. I handed you the tools, I helped you do awful things, I learned how to use the shock machine, and you repaid me by experimenting on me too. My surgery was the most successful of all, you said. You were so pleased about your work as I grew up and made you proud. But on that day, you took away the basic things a person requires to exist. There's only a shred left — a particle of remembrance about right and wrong, good and evil. You didn't take enough, Father. You left a tiny shred for me to cling to, and that was a mistake.

Craig stood like a mannequin for several minutes. Landry and Cate watched in silence as he stared into some faraway place deep in his thoughts. Perhaps he saw people there — his people — or maybe he was contemplating the consequences of his actions. This wasn't a lapse; he was just lost in thought. In a moment he snapped back. He stretched, yawned and said, "You're right. It's time to end all this."

CHAPTER THIRTY-THREE

In an ideal world, Landry would have let Craig talk right then, but he needed to record this. He'd snapped a few photos at Amelia House, but he needed much more before this story became a television episode. Plus, he still wasn't certain Craig would allow it. Landry had to be careful, and caution wasn't a dominant trait of his.

Summoning the patience to do this the correct way, he asked Craig if they could record an interview at his studio in New Orleans. To his surprise, he agreed, saying the sooner he got out of Jeanerette, the better. They accompanied him to return the truck he'd borrowed, and the three of them drove to the Big Easy. On the way he called his pilot and arranged a pickup in New Orleans later in the week. Ready to put things behind him, he asked to do the interview as soon as possible. Landry called the station, told Ted what was up, and he agreed to assemble a production team and have a studio ready by three.

Craig rented a suite at the Ritz-Carlton on Canal, and when they dropped him off, they agreed to meet at M Bistro in the hotel for lunch. It had a special feature that would come in handy — something known as a cheater's booth.

Two recognizable people having lunch — one of the richest men ever to come out of Louisiana and a famous paranormal investigator — would attract attention and questions. The last thing Landry wanted was for some well-meaning fellow guest to approach their table and spook Craig.

He and Cate unloaded the Jeep and walked through the Quarter to the Ritz. They met Craig, and the maître d' seated them, drawing a curtain across the front of the booth to give them privacy.

Cate was with them. After experiencing some of this adventure, she couldn't stop now. Landry talked about the shoot. He explained how things worked, how many audio and video people would be in the studio, and how he'd moderate the session. Craig had done live interviews for CNBC and MSNBC when he sold his company, but today would be new for him. Cable news segments were typically one to three minutes. Today's might run ninety minutes or longer, which would edit down to maybe twenty minutes of footage.

Craig had asked for a list of questions in advance, but Landry said he didn't do it that way. The answers needed to be fresh, not rehearsed, and since the show was taped, mistakes would be edited out.

They arrived at Channel 9, Landry introduced Craig to everyone, and they walked into the studio. As the director placed them in chairs across a glass table from each other, Craig brought up something new.

This late in the game, he demanded the right to edit content. If he wasn't happy later on with something he'd said, they'd have to remove it.

Exasperated, Landry wondered if the interview would happen after all. He wasn't going to give Craig what he wanted, and he explained why not.

THE EXPERIMENTS: THE BAYOU HAUNTING 5

"You've said it's time to end all this. I'll ask leading questions designed to strike at your emotions. I don't put people on the spot, or turn hostile in the middle of an interview, or delve into private matters that are off-subject. But I do probe and push to coax heartfelt answers that help our viewers understand why and how things happened. Once you've committed not to hide things anymore, you can trust me to help you tell the story."

"What if I'm charged with murder?"

"From what I know, that won't happen. Your parents forced you to help with operations when you were a kid. You never saw your parents get rid of a victim. No reasonable person would hold you responsible for those things. In 2003 you took possession of three bodies and hid them in a closet. That was almost twenty years ago, and you broke a state law that says you have to bury the deceased. They won't charge you now. If they did, it's not a capital offense, so if you've told me everything, I think you have nothing to worry about."

Craig thought about that answer longer than Landry would have expected. A few times he started to ask a question, but then he backed off. At last he said he was ready to proceed. At a few minutes past three they sat on opposite sides of a glass desk. Landry's director counted down from five, pointed his finger, and the interview began.

CHAPTER THIRTY-FOUR

To make things easier for Craig, Landry began with topics they'd discussed earlier. Craig told about his childhood, the secret about having a brother, the locked doors, the laboratory and the dumbwaiter.

Once they finished that segment, a picture of the mausoleum appeared on a large screen behind Landry and Craig. "Let's look at these," Landry began, guiding Craig as he identified his relatives one by one and explained how they were part of the story of Amelia House.

Craig related his family's history as his relatives had passed it down through the generations. His great-grandfather began experimenting on people because he had had a noble passion to turn bad people into good ones. Later things changed. They still claimed to be looking for answers, but the Morissets became sadistic killers. They played with men's brains, kept detailed notes, and then eliminated them.

"Did you read those notes?"

"Yes. Marco built a building in the woods everyone called the laboratory, but it wasn't that. It's where they did research. He kept meticulous records in notebooks. One case might cover hundreds of pages, including how he found the patient, what it took to lure him to the house, how they anesthetized him, and details of the procedure. They recorded his progress all the way to the end, when they outlined his death and wrote down what they did with the remains."

"That must have been a terrible revelation for you."

"Devastating. I read the first victim's account page for page. He was a hobo who chose the wrong back door to knock on for a handout back in 1909. I read every horrifying detail on him, but not the rest. There were just too many, and on the others I'd skim the highlights and skip the details. I became jaded — I decided other people must have relatives who did bad things too. I never dared tell anyone about what I read, because I didn't want other kids to brand my family as — well, as what they were."

Craig described in gruesome detail the operations his ancestors called leukotomies, what they entailed, and exactly how they did them. Then he talked about how easy it was in those days for someone to get a medical license and how his grandfather's was revoked.

"Albert came close to breaching the unwritten Morisset law — never reveal the secrets that go on inside Amelia House. Looking for peer recognition, he published articles in medical journals that he termed theories. Who would have known they were true? He talked about altering the mind to create a good man from an evil one, but he omitted the fact that he and his father had been trying it for years.

"Instead of praising him, his peers accused him of playing God and pressured the medical board to take away his license. They thought he was crazy. Just how crazy, no one could have imagined."

He explained how Marco and Albert procured and studied their victims. Albert took advantage of World War II. He and his wife offered free room and board for returning soldiers while they looked for jobs. The ones who had families went on their ways, but men with no place to go eventually found themselves strapped to a metal table inside Amelia House.

Landry asked about Craig's parents. He was intimately familiar with their operations, explaining how his father groomed him to take over the family business. He forced Craig to hold the instruments and watch the procedures.

"They also groomed your brother, correct? I don't think townspeople ever knew he existed."

"Yes. Jerry was my half-brother and fifteen years older, which made him strong enough to do the physical labor required for the procedures. Sometimes he held the men down while my mother held the electrodes to their temples. Afterwards he carted bodies to the family mausoleum in the Jeanerette cemetery. The empty crypts there are stuffed with victims."

Landry hadn't expected Craig to disclose that so early, and it had a jarring effect on those in the room. His jaded director, who thought he'd heard everything, stared in disbelief at the notion they hid the bodies in their own mausoleum.

Landry continued. "If the men died during the operations, how could that benefit the research your parents purported to be undertaking?"

"No one died *during* an operation. A lobotomy is a simple, almost painless ten-minute procedure. The men came out from under the anesthetic able to walk and talk like before, but my relatives couldn't risk locking the victims up for long periods of time. They'd snatch a victim, hold him prisoner for a day or so, do their dirty work, keep him alive a day more, and inject him with a hypodermic full of air. I learned from reading the files that eventually they were performing surgeries for their own sadistic gratification and not for scientific research."

Those listening wondered how this could have gone on for years in a small town and no one suspected anything.

This interview was hard to believe, yet without emotion, a family member explained the details that branded his own parents as kidnappers and murderers.

There was a collective sigh of relief when Landry changed topics. He said, "I'm sure people in south Louisiana will remember the fire that killed your parents in 2003. Tell me about that."

When Craig didn't answer, Landry looked up from his notes and saw him descending into a fugue. "Keep the camera on him," he whispered to the director. "Don't miss any of this."

Craig spoke tonelessly as his eyes focused on something far away.

No, Mother. I'm going to tell them the rest. You can't stop me any longer. After helping him with strangers, you turned on your own child. You told Father to operate on me because I knew too much about you both. You said if he'd do it, I wouldn't remember, and I wouldn't be a danger to the family any longer. If he took my memories away, I wouldn't be able to tell the truth and expose my parents.

The operation worked for many years, because I forgot almost everything. Only a few of the horrible things you both did remained in my memory. But when I came back to Amelia House, everything seeped into my mind like raw sewage. I remembered about Marco and Albert and you and Father. All of you were nothing more than ruthless, demented killers.

I was still a teenager when I started my company, and it became an instant success. You took credit for that. You thought my lobotomy was your crowning achievement. Along with erasing your heinous sins from my mind, you created a financial genius. But you did neither. I regained the awful memories you thought you erased, and I earned success through a little hard work and a lot of luck. It was my achievement, not yours.

He paused as if listening, and then he continued.

THE EXPERIMENTS: THE BAYOU HAUNTING 5

You don't understand. I don't care what they do to me. You can't reach me, you can't stop me, and I won't be part of your coverup anymore. No more protecting the Morissets. It all ends today.

The studio was as silent as the proverbial tomb as they watched Craig return. He blinked his eyes, looked around the room, and took a moment to orient himself.

"I guess that must have been revealing," he said at last. "I don't want to hear about it. Just keep going."

"Before we resume, I have a favor to ask," Landry said. "It's critical that I take a film crew to Amelia House. I'd like for you to be there too. I'll understand if you don't want to come, but I have to get video inside the house to make your story more real to our viewers."

Craig nodded. "What you say makes sense. There's nothing more to hide, so you can go. I might come too. I'll think about that. Now let's get this over with."

"While you were away from us a few minutes ago, you revealed that you underwent a lobotomy yourself."

"I said that? Play it back for me."

They paused while the audio technician located the segment and replayed it. Craig said, "It's all true. They hoped to erase my memory so I couldn't do this — reveal the secrets. I don't want to talk about that. Let's take a break."

Craig walked to a corner and leaned back in a chair with his eyes closed. Cate wanted to go see about him, but Landry said no. This had to be as traumatic as helping with the gruesome experiments had been, and Landry thought Craig needed time with his thoughts.

When they returned, Landry walked Craig through the fire that killed his parents and brother. He explained about the outbuilding in the woods, and he said something Landry hadn't heard earlier.

"The laboratory had no windows, and it had way more insulation in the walls and ceilings than a typical building."

"Why?"

"Because a long time ago it was for more than research. It also had twelve cells."

"It had cells?"

"Yes, like holding cells in a jail. When I first went in the laboratory, I knew what they'd done. They kept victims there until they were ready to do the surgeries. I figured there would have been a lot of screaming and shouting, and that's why my great-grandfather built it with no windows and lots of soundproofing."

"Did you ever see a patient locked up in there?"

"No. By the time I was old enough to steal the key and go inside, they were using the cells for storage. But I felt things when I went in there. I'd be reading Marco's or Albert's notes about a procedure and I'd get this eerie feeling I wasn't alone. When it happened, I ran away, but something always brought me back. I wanted to know everything about my family, no matter how horrible it was. I'm a Morisset too, you know.

"My father and mother made me go fetch things from there sometimes. They knew exactly which box contained certain notes they wanted, and they'd tell me which cell it was in. When I went inside a cell, I would prop the door open with a chair, because I had this strange feeling that it would slam closed, lock me in, and I'd die there because my parents wouldn't ever come to check on me."

Landry switched gears again, this time to what he planned as the climax for his show. After everything so far, viewers would learn the astounding story of how Craig returned after the fire and locked three bodies in the house instead of burying them in the family mausoleum.

He couldn't have known that even he was about to be astounded, because there was far more to this story than Landry could have imagined.

CHAPTER THIRTY-FIVE

"Let's talk about the day of the fire. You told me earlier you were in Lafayette."

"Yes," he said, explaining how he got the call and later returned to Jeanerette to claim the bodies.

"What caused the fire?"

"They used ethyl alcohol in their operations. It's highly flammable and was stored outside the building, and somehow it ignited. With my family inside, the fire marshal decided one of them started it, and he determined their deaths to be accidental."

"There are crypts in the family mausoleum that bear the names of your parents, but no marker with the name of your brother, Jerry. Why is that?"

Again Craig paused, and again Landry signaled to keep things rolling as they watched him drift away.

He mumbled something and cocked his head. He clinched his fists and contorted his face into a grimace, and as quickly as it started, the trance ended with a single sentence.

You can't stop me, and it doesn't matter what they do to me now.

He stared at Landry for a few seconds and said, "You asked about the bodies, right?"

Landry nodded and waited for the answer he expected. Instead, Craig had another bombshell for him.

"I have a confession. I've always said I was in Lafayette when the fire started. I made up that lie so long ago that I almost believed it myself. I even said it to you a moment ago, but now it's time to set the record straight.

"I was in Jeanerette, not Lafayette. I went to Amelia House, locked them inside the laboratory, doused the place with ethyl alcohol, and set it ablaze. I killed them — all three of them."

Holy shit, someone shouted from the shadows behind the huge lights that illuminated the set. There were gasps of disbelief and the sounds of people talking.

The director stormed over to the table, turned to his cameramen, sound guys and the few assembled guests, and shouted, "Dammit, we're taping a segment here! You people are professionals, so knock off the theatrics. You visitors, either shut up or get the hell out!" As he walked back to his chair, he decided *holy shit* was an accurate term for what just happened, but he had to keep things moving, no matter what. The more revelations, the better the show. And this one just might be one for the books.

Hoping the disruption hadn't made Craig lose his nerve, Landry said, "You're saying you set the laboratory on fire?"

"Yes. I drove to Jeanerette to murder them. It was good fortune that they were all inside. I barricaded the doors and emptied the drums of alcohol around the foundation. The place was an inferno within seconds, and I knew no one could survive. From my perspective, it couldn't have turned out better."

Landry was flustered. It never happened during an interview, and he was caught off guard. He shuffled papers and struggled to collect his thoughts.

THE EXPERIMENTS: THE BAYOU HAUNTING 5

What questions do I ask next? How do I steer this for maximum effect?

This interview was pure dynamite — a journalist's dream. What a newsman wouldn't do to have a subject confess on camera to capital crimes, and today it happened. He had to keep firing questions. With Craig primed and ready to bare his soul, all Landry had to do was push the right buttons.

From the back of the studio, Ted had watched everything. When Craig confessed, he stepped out.

Landry continued. "Okay, so you're saying you left and then returned when you got the call about the fire. Is that an accurate statement?"

"Yes. I told my assistant not to disturb me, and I left my office through a back door. I drove to Jeanerette, set the fire, and waited long enough to be sure I'd done what I came for. Then I headed south and took a farm road off the main highway. I found a shady spot near the river and waited. I remember it being around fifteen minutes before someone connected Amelia House to me and called the office. My assistant called me on my cell, and I waited forty-five more minutes before I drove to the house and met the fire marshal."

"And he had no reason to suspect your involvement?"

Craig nodded.

"You told him you were at your office in Lafayette. How far from your house is that?"

"Forty miles. Nobody checked my alibi. At the time my parents started the fire, I was at my office. They spilled the alcohol and burned themselves to death. Who'd suspect a successful twenty-three-year-old multimillionaire running a company he created?"

"And this is the first time you've revealed the truth?"

He nodded. "I've never admitted it to anyone. Like I said earlier, you lie about something long enough and you begin to believe it yourself."

"Are you concerned about the consequences of this confession?"

"I've lived with this for seventeen years. Someday everyone has to face the consequences of his actions. Today's my day."

"And regrets?"

For some reason, that question appeared to set Craig off. He glanced up in surprise as though the thought had never entered his mind, and then he sneered, "Regrets? Are you kidding? Have you listened to anything I said? They should erect a statue to me in the town square."

To ease the tone, he switched subjects again. "A little earlier I asked you about the bodies of your parents and brother. The Morisset mausoleum sits in the Jeanerette cemetery. There's no marker for your brother, Jerry. Why is that?"

In a congenial voice he replied, "The markers for my parents were already in place. My father had them made when he buried his own parents, knowing he and Mother would end up there someday. I didn't order a faceplate for Jerry because I never intended to bury him there."

"What did you do instead?"

"None of the three bodies are in their crypts. When the medical examiner ruled the deaths accidental, I had the bodies delivered to Amelia House, and that's where they are today."

This time the room exploded. Everybody talked at once and the director shouted, "Are you f-ing kidding me? Landry, we're done here. We're way, way out of our league on this one. We have to call the cops."

Ted Carpenter walked out of the dark recesses of the studio, accompanied by two officers. He said, "I called the police after Craig confessed. Detective, it's all yours from here."

A detective with the New Orleans Police Department introduced himself as Shane Young and said, "Mr.

THE EXPERIMENTS: THE BAYOU HAUNTING 5

Morisset, I understand that while being interviewed and recorded, you confessed to several crimes this afternoon. Do you wish to continue speaking with Mr. Drake? It's your prerogative to stop at any time, and it's my duty to inform you that you're going to be arrested when this is over. If you want to keep going, I'll read you your rights now and Mr. Drake can proceed with his questioning. We'll stay in the room to take you into custody at the end. Anything you have said on tape, or that you say going forward, can and will be used against you in a court of law."

Landry held his breath. He couldn't predict what avenue Craig would choose, but a selfish part of him hoped it would go on. By any measurement, this was one of the bombshell interviews of a reporter's life, and it would make one hell of a *Bayou Hauntings* episode.

His head a maze of churning thoughts, Craig sat with his shoulders slumped. Everything that had been real two hours before was upended now. Never again would his life be the same. His boat in Key Largo, the plane, the idyllic life near the water, the things he had accumulated while living a lie — all of it vanished with a few truthful statements.

Now that he'd come clean, he resigned himself to take whatever he had coming. He couldn't predict what would happen after today, but he deserved anything the authorities wanted to do.

The most amazing thought that crossed his mind was that all this didn't have to happen. If he hadn't returned to Jeanerette — if he'd kept his promise to himself and never come home — no one would be the wiser.

"Read me the rights," he said. "I'm not finished yet."

The detective did so, and he asked Landry's director to check the equipment and ensure the conversation was being recorded.

That done, the interview began again. "We left off with your saying the bodies of Frank, Maria and Jerry Morisset are in Amelia House today."

Craig stopped him. "One correction. Jerry's last name isn't Morisset. It's Oubre, my mother's maiden name. He's my half-brother — the child of my mother but not my father. My father refused to adopt him because he was a bastard."

That might have surprised the ones in the room if so much hadn't been dropped on them already. The insane father wouldn't make the boy his own. Instead he made Jerry the operating room assistant, and then he lobotomized him. Bizarre didn't properly describe this family. The word *evil* fit better.

"Where inside Amelia House are the three bodies?"

"I put them in the back of a closet in my parents' bedroom in 2003. They were still there two weeks ago when I came back to Iberia Parish for my class reunion."

"And how do you know they were still there?"

"Because I found them upstairs. The moment I set foot in that house, something swept over me, compelling me to go to that locked closet and let them out. It was an overpowering sensation I couldn't resist if I'd tried. But I didn't try. I've explained that the family's blood runs in my veins. I wanted to go there. Somehow by putting them in that closet, I imprisoned them. I can't tell you how it happened — I can't explain anything about them — but once I opened the door, I also broke the spell and freed them. They still roam that house today."

Landry had witnessed most of what he would be asking next. He thought he knew the answers, but after the shocking revelations so far, there was no telling what else they might learn.

"I saw your parents' bodies when I was in the house. They were badly burned — recognizable as having been human only by their shapes. Was that how they were when the medical examiner released them to you?"

"Yes. By the time the fire crew arrived, the flames had spread everywhere. Two bodies were burned beyond recognition, but not Jerry's. Since 2003 I hadn't understood why, but when I was there two weeks ago, he told me."

It was another startling revelation for the people in the room, but not for Landry, who understood him. For effect, he feigned ignorance.

"He told you? You said a few minutes ago he died in 2003. How could he tell you something seventeen years later? Jerry *is* dead, correct?"

"Yes. He died of smoke inhalation in the fire."

"So he's dead, but he spoke to you."

"Father never realized that while poking around in Jerry's brain, he triggered something unique. He managed to alter the physical concept of death. You saw him, Landry. The only way to describe him is *undead*. He doesn't look like a zombie or a swamp creature. His body never deteriorated, and in a way his mind still works, even though it's more twisted and demented now than when he was alive. From a physiological and mental standpoint, he's changed, but his outward appearance is the same as on that day in 2003. He died, but he *didn't* die."

Detective Young listened from the back of the room, thinking that this had to be the most unusual case he would ever see, and now it just got crazier. The victim's dead, but he isn't, so would a jury convict Craig of killing him? They had two other bodies and a taped confession. He hoped that was enough to send this joker to the death chamber.

CHAPTER THIRTY-SIX

During a short break, the director congratulated Landry on how well things were going. Rarely did an investigator have the good fortune to be an eyewitness, and his personal backstory would be added before this show aired. Although Craig's words were the bombshells, Landry's would add meat to the bones of this bizarre tale.

Landry walked across the room and sat down next to Cate, who echoed the director's comments. "Wow, this one will blow your fans away. Once this episode airs, we won't be able to go anywhere without your groupies mobbing you."

He laughed. "I guess it's time to interview bodyguards, although I think I'll hold off at first. I want to see how it feels to have teenaged girls fainting at the sight of me."

"Don't get a big head. You're *my* rock star, not theirs."

When Landry returned to the set, the interview resumed. He brought up the morning when they were in Jeanerette. "Do you remember seeing me at the house? I was in the office and you were standing in the corner. You spoke to me, but somehow you disappeared. I didn't know at the time how you managed that, but I believe now you rode the dumbwaiter upstairs."

Craig said he didn't recall Landry's being there.

"That's because you were in one of your trances. What happened to you inside the house?"

He described going into the bedroom he hadn't seen in seventeen years and finding the bodies where he'd left them.

"When I opened that closet door, I unleashed something supernatural. I released them from a dormancy — the finality of death that we expect the deceased to embrace. How ironic that my staying away kept them leashed, but my homecoming set them free."

That was a good segue into that Saturday when the five of them stayed at the house. First, they talked about the reason Craig returned to Louisiana — the ceremony at St. Anne's University — and his decision to attend the reunion parties. When the hurricane came their way, they drove to Amelia House.

Craig described how they settled into the old house, dealt with sporadic power outages, found outdated cans of food that the doctor proclaimed edible, and built a roaring fire. On Saturday afternoon his family captured their next victim — one of Craig's friends, and he decided he must stop them.

When they took another break, Craig asked to use the restroom. Detective Young handcuffed the other cop and Craig together, and they left the room.

Cate came over and said, "Is that necessary? He won't run away. Just look at him. He's a broken man."

Young disagreed. "You have no idea what he is. He killed his parents and his brother, and so far I haven't heard a word of remorse or regret. He's a cold-blooded murderer, and if this guy escaped, the shit comes down on me. I'm already thinking I should end this and take him downtown, but I want to be sure we've heard everything he wants to say. Landry, you're doing a better job than our interrogators could, but we need to get this wrapped up soon."

When Craig and the deputy returned, they continued.

"When your friends and I were at Amelia House, did you see your parents?"

"No, not then."

Landry talked about going to the house alone and encountering Craig's brother, Jerry, who pretended to be the caretaker. They discussed what happened in the laboratory, the vines that wrapped Landry into a cocoon, and how he had been next in line for a lobotomy. Landry acknowledged that by flying back from Florida and coming to the house, Craig had saved his life.

"Now and then you enter a state of paramnesia that you call a lapse, correct?"

"Yes, even today. I don't realize it when I lapse, but afterwards sometimes it's obvious by how people react."

"You said that they started on January 24, 1989. How can you pinpoint the exact day?"

"They began on the day I got a lobotomy. January the twenty-fourth."

"How old were you?"

"Ten. I didn't know what my parents were planning. I thought it was just another surgery. I hated helping, but I had no choice. They ordered me to assist in the laboratory, but when I walked in, there was no patient. Jerry was twenty-five and much bigger than me. He and my father pinned me to the table, my mother applied the electrodes, and I woke up later."

"A few years after that you created KeenLock, which you sold for three-quarters of a billion dollars. Your parents believed they were responsible for your success because of the lobotomy."

"Yes, but it had to remain a secret, because otherwise everything would blow up in their faces. My father and mother didn't want to be physicians. They preferred to do their work behind the scenes, away from the realm of peer reviews and license revocation hearings. Their victims never filed a malpractice claim, or ran to the news media, or threatened a lawsuit. They were the unfortunates, many of whose names they never knew. My parents operated, then eliminated, and Jerry took them to the mausoleum at night."

"Why did you…was there any significance to the exact day you decided to, uh, as you call it…*eliminate* your family?"

"It happened the day I admitted to myself that if I didn't do something, this would never end. The Morisset men had been playing doctor — and God — since the early nineteen hundreds. Each of them taught his son the trade and every one became a murderer.

"My father groomed Jerry to be his successor, and he tried to get me too, but I escaped by going off to school. When I set the fire in 2003, my father was sixty-seven and Jerry was thirty-eight. They were in good health, and they would have continued this killing spree until they died or got caught — which was always a possibility when you were in their business. It could have continued for decades.

"That day in 2003 when I came home, I wasn't sure if the opportunity would present itself. But it did; they were out in the field laboratory, comparing notes, writing reports, whatever they did. I went straight to work, and it was all over in twenty minutes."

"One last question. How were your parents and Jerry resurrected? You say you 'unleashed them,' but what allowed them to return from the dead?"

"That's something I'll never be sure of. Every Morisset man was fascinated with the human brain. One of them discovered how to alter the dying process — not to make a person live again, but to keep them from being completely dead. My concern now isn't how it happened. I stopped them once, and now I must do it again, because they're still inside Amelia House."

CHAPTER THIRTY-SEVEN

The filming ended, the director called it a wrap, and Detective Young handcuffed Craig. Curious if Craig would post bail, Landry asked what the charges would be. Arson and first-degree murder was his answer, which meant to Landry that Craig wouldn't be out anytime soon.

Craig gave Landry the number of his attorney, a former congressman in Baton Rouge. He wasn't a criminal lawyer, but since money was no object, Craig trusted the man to hire the best people possible. Landry promised to call him and keep in touch.

After everyone left, Ted pulled Landry aside and said, "I hope you understand that I had to call the police. When he began that story —"

"I understand. I'm just glad they let me finish the interview. I feel sorry for him, and that's why I promised to keep in touch."

Ted said, "His lawyer's one of the most powerful men in the state. With the money he has, there's no telling who his criminal attorney will be. It's critical that you stay in contact with him. If there's more to this story, hopefully you'll be the first to know. You've already got a blockbuster episode coming together."

Landry agreed. "Before we started today, I thought we were onto something big, and then he threw out one surprise after another. He's a tormented person whose family put him through a kind of hell we can't imagine. I'm glad I witnessed supernatural activity at the house, and if his story is true, I'm not surprised he killed them. My God, Ted. They were monsters."

He called the former senator and gave him a brief version of his client's predicament. He promised to get right on it and took Landry's number. Thirty minutes later a New Orleans attorney named Pamela Sacriste called and set up a meeting for tomorrow morning. She promised nothing, saying she wanted to talk about his situation before she committed.

It was only a few blocks from Channel Nine's studio to the Sacriste Law Firm's office on the nineteenth floor of a Poydras Street building. He waited in a conference room until a woman in her early forties came in, shook hands and sat across the table. Dressed in black, her demeanor was all business. He decided if he ever ended up like Craig, she looked like a good one to hire.

She shot questions his way for an hour, never raising an eyebrow or giving him a quizzical look as he explained about Craig and the segment they'd taped yesterday. She made notes, listened to every word, and spoke only when Landry finished.

"That's an amazing account," the lawyer said. "I respect you, Mr. Drake. I've followed your investigative reporting, and to tell you the truth, if you hadn't witnessed some of these bizarre events, I'd advise Mr. Morisset to find a different attorney and make up a better story."

"It's a bizarre tale," Landry agreed, "but it's all true. Will you help him?"

THE EXPERIMENTS: THE BAYOU HAUNTING 5

"I'm not sure yet. If I accept him as a client, I'll have a professional evaluate his mental state. Let me ask you a question. If the prosecutor asked you under oath whether you believe he was insane, how would you answer? I'm sure you realize they will surely call you to testify, because you're right in the middle of all this. Speaking of which, how about that confession you drug out of him? Don't answer that. I'm sounding like his lawyer already, and that certainly isn't a foregone conclusion. Off the record, what's your opinion? Is Craig Morisset crazy?"

"He experienced paranormal things, and to some people that would make him crazy. He admits to horrific crimes, but he had a good reason. Sure, his story is bizarre, but I believe every word. I saw a lot of it myself. Does that make him crazy, or me, or both of us?"

"When you're in a courtroom, who knows? It doesn't surprise me that you accept his story, because you're a professional ghost hunter. The prosecution would love you because you'd testify that he was as sane as the next guy. Would it come to that? Who knows?"

She stood and extended her hand. "Thanks for your help. I'll be in touch."

Landry said, "He needs the best attorney he can get."

Sacriste nodded. "That's an understatement."

Back at Channel Nine, Landry googled her name and saw that she was one of the most successful criminal defense attorneys in the South. She had won acquittal in several high-profile cases Landry remembered. Pamela Sacriste was a highly regarded attorney and a tenacious advocate for her clients.

Around ten the next morning Landry received word that Pamela Sacriste was Craig's attorney of record. Now that he knew, he was ready to implement his plan. Yesterday Craig had agreed to allow a film crew into the house, but that was before his arrest. Landry needed much more than permission now.

Prior to his interview, it would have been easy. Craig could call the maintenance company in Jeanerette, and someone would let Landry and his people in. But the house was a crime scene now. Soon the cops would swarm the building, gathering evidence and information to either substantiate or refute Craig's astonishing assertions of what happened there. But Landry had another idea, a long shot that just might work.

He called Pamela Sacriste, explained his proposal, and was pleased to hear she liked it. Although unconventional, it could serve a purpose for everyone involved, if she could sell it to the authorities.

Two hours later Pamela and Landry sat in the visitor's room of the New Orleans jail, looking through a reinforced-glass window at a defeated, humble man.

Here sits living proof that money can't solve all your problems, although it can buy you a damned good lawyer.

Landry outlined his idea to Craig, who liked it. Not only did he have nothing to lose, what Landry proposed just might convince the authorities and the world that his astonishing story was true.

The easy hurdle completed, Landry and Pamela turned next to the New Orleans Police Department. Landry's request was so unconventional that it would require approval from the very top, and Pamela had the number on speed dial.

Not only was she the city's top criminal defense attorney, she was also a well-connected and very generous contributor to political races. Through both avenues, she had become friends with the chief of police. That afternoon she and Landry walked into his office, where she got a hug and a peck on the cheek, while Landry got a hearty handshake.

"I'm a huge fan of yours, Landry," the chief declared. "My life is all about facts, so there's never room for off-the-wall ideas. I can escape in your *Bayou Hauntings*

THE EXPERIMENTS: THE BAYOU HAUNTING

shows. Between you and me, is any of that stuff on your show real?"

"All of it. We don't alter any of the audio or video you see on TV. I see more evidence every day that the paranormal not only exists, but it flourishes in the right environments, like the old houses and buildings I've investigated."

"Well, I'm pleased to get to meet you. Pam, to what do I owe this honor?"

"Craig Morisset's being held without bond in your jail, as I'm sure you're aware."

"Yeah. He's only been here twenty-four hours, and already I've fielded calls from every media outlet in the state. I don't know much about his case, only that he's charged with murdering his family nearly twenty years ago. Are you his attorney? If so, it's not appropriate for you to be here."

"I am, but I think you'll agree we're fine. I didn't come to discuss his case. Mr. Drake came to me with a far-fetched idea I liked enough to bring to you. I'm asking you to hear him out."

Landry summarized everything that had happened since his arrival in Iberia Parish that Thursday two weeks ago, explained his proposal, and asked the chief to approve his request.

The chief only asked a couple of questions during Landry's spiel, and afterwards he told Pamela the story was fascinating, but even more so because Landry had observed parts of it himself. He winked at Landry and said, "Whatever happens, this is going to be the best show you've ever produced!"

Regarding the request, he said he would talk to the attorney general and let Pam know. He explained, "Craig's being held in New Orleans because he confessed here. The alleged crimes occurred in Iberia Parish, and I expect Miss Sacriste will ask for a transfer."

She smiled but said nothing.

"She's as forthcoming as always, I see," he quipped, and she laughed. "Anyway, Craig's case is already getting national attention, and I don't know where he'll end up. I have to inform the AG up front about what you're asking. If he goes for it, then you've got a deal."

It was hard for Landry to accomplish much over the next two days. The time dragged by, and with every passing hour he felt less optimistic that the attorney general would approve his idea. It was far-fetched for sure. Unprecedented too, most likely. But it had little downside and a lot of potential gain, especially for Craig. As a suspect in several capital offenses, he deserved every opportunity to clear his name. In the end, that last point convinced the state of Louisiana's top lawyer to give his blessing.

CHAPTER THIRTY-EIGHT

Anyone who watched the convoy pass might suppose the governor was on his way to a meeting. By order of the attorney general, four state police Suburbans, their flashing blue lights piercing the nighttime skies, drove from New Orleans to Jeanerette.

The first vehicle held a state police driver, NOPD Detective Young and two New Orleans cops. Craig sat in the back seat of the second SUV, his hands cuffed and ankle shackles hooked to a ring in the floorboard. Four police officers rode in his car — the driver, one in the passenger seat and two in the back, one on either side of Craig.

Cate, Landry, his director, cameraman Phil Vandegriff, a gaffer and a sound man were in the third car. Last was another Suburban, this one filled with broadcasting equipment.

When they arrived at Amelia House around nine p.m., the Jeanerette chief of police and Iberia Parish sheriff were waiting. Police cruisers blocked the long driveway, and local officers waved the convoy through. Everyone else was off-limits while the prisoner was on premises.

Per Craig's instructions to the management company, the house was unlocked, and policemen fanned out to secure every room. Meanwhile, Landry's crew set up everything and started the cameras rolling before the cops reported back to Detective Young that there were three locked rooms on the top floor.

Young asked Craig for a key, and he revealed where he'd hidden them. Cameras followed them to the third floor and into the closet of Craig's childhood bedroom. On the back of a rafter in the closet they found a ring with three keys, the set Craig stole as a child. Landry handed them to Detective Young as Craig explained that one was the bedroom of Craig's parents, the second was his brother Jerry's room, and the last was the laboratory where most of the paranormal activity in the house had occurred.

"The ghosts of his family are still within these walls," Landry said, and two of the cops gave nervous chuckles. "This is no joke," he snapped. "That middle room's the most haunted part of the entire house."

The detective told his men to work in pairs, staying in those locked rooms just long enough to be sure they were empty. Despite the seriousness of the situation, Landry smiled as the cops who had snickered now cowered behind their flashlights and crept into the dark laboratory.

Everything was quiet. It wouldn't have surprised Landry if they'd found Craig's family, but their absence didn't mean he had failed. He only hoped they'd show up before their visit was over.

Landry's plan was to recreate a past visit to the laboratory. Like a director at a rehearsal, he told his players where to stand, what to do, things to watch for, and the starring role Craig would be playing. They had to keep him safe — not just because he was an accused felon, but because his willingness to come back to the house might put his life in danger. Whether a bunch of no-nonsense cops believed it or not.

THE EXPERIMENTS: THE BAYOU HAUNTING 5

Phil put three motion-activated cameras in the laboratory — two in corners and one pointed toward the metal table in the middle. Other cameras would capture motion in the hallways, and there were more in the bedroom and the office where the dumbwaiter opened. A monitor in the hallway displayed the feeds from all the cameras, and that was where some of those present would watch things play out on the screens.

The fewer people in the laboratory, the better, although the detective told Landry Craig could not be alone. A young NOPD officer handcuffed Craig's wrist to his own as Craig unlocked the door. They went in, closed it and stood in a dark corner to wait. Three other officers waited in the hall just outside the door. If there came a cry for help, they would rush into the room, turn on the lights, and deal with the situation.

For the camera, Landry would ride the dumbwaiter from the ground floor to the top. He didn't relish crawling back in that cramped box, but he needed it for the show.

He took the Jeanerette police chief and the sheriff downstairs to the office. He showed them how the panel opened and the dumbwaiter worked. He took a set of wired walkie-talkies from his backpack, gave the sheriff one, and he strung wire into the dumbwaiter. He stepped inside, connected the wire to his unit and hung it inside the car. It was voice-activated; when they tested it, everything Landry said came through loud and clear on the sheriff's unit. If something went wrong while he was inside, the men would rescue Landry, whatever it took.

He slid the panel shut, pressed the button, and the machine started up. At the top, Landry put his palm on the panel and slid it to one side. It opened easily, and he whispered, "I'm going into the laboratory now."

The broken window had been repaired and the black curtain rehung, so that the room was once again enveloped in darkness. Landry turned on his flashlight and played it around the room. He saw Craig and the officer standing in the opposite corner and he moved on, ending up where he'd first seen the charred corpses. The screen was where it had been, and he crossed the room and stood in front of it. With a shiver of apprehension, he grabbed it and moved it aside in one quick thrust. It wouldn't have surprised him to find two shriveled bodies, but the chairs were empty.

Landry shone the light on a tray beside the metal table. There were surgical instruments neatly arranged for an operation. At the head of the table was something he'd missed before — a rectangular wooden box with its lid open. Inside were gears and old-fashioned batteries, and two metal electrodes ran from wires connected to the sides of the box. He raised his eyebrows, pointed at the box, and glanced in Craig's direction. There came a whisper. "It's an electroconvulsive shock machine, for anesthetizing the patients."

The apparatus had a hand crank to power up the batteries before electricity was in common use. Today a cord ran to a plug in the wall.

He switched it on, listened to the soft whirr of the batteries as they powered up, and touched the electrodes. His fingertips tingled as he felt a current, and he turned a dial on the machine, increasing the shock until it was too painful to touch.

"Landry!" came Craig's sharp whisper. "Watch out!"

With his attention focused on the old device, he hadn't noticed the vines sweeping across the floor. Now he felt them encircling his feet. When he tried to kick them away, they drew tighter, just as before.

"Leave him alone!" Craig shouted. "You promised you wouldn't take him!"

A curious mixture of sounds swirled like a tempest above Landry's head. He heard childish laughter, groans of agony, snippets of sentences that made no sense — a

THE EXPERIMENTS: THE BAYOU HAUNTING 5

cacophony of noise echoing off the walls of the laboratory. And then there was a familiar voice.

"Leave him alone? But, brother, you brought him back to us. He's ours now."

"You can have the others. Or me. But not him. He's my friend. He tried to help me. You promised —"

Jerry emerged from somewhere in the shadows and stood at the head of the metal table, mere feet away from Landry, who was struggling against the vines that were now above his knees. In the dim light from the phone Landry saw the look of glee on his face.

He spewed out a horrible, maniacal laugh. "Friend? Don't deceive yourself, little brother. This man isn't your friend. We Morissets never had friends, remember? And no one's off-limits in the name of medical science. The table's waiting for your friend!"

Jerking at the handcuffs, Craig pulled the officer along until he found the light switch. When the globes above the table illuminated, the astonished cop found Landry entwined in tendrils that extended almost to his waist. He noticed others in the room too — Jerry, who appeared to be a living being, and two black shapes that had once been humans. Fear rushed over him in waves as he screamed for help.

Jerry cackled with delight as people from the hall began banging on the door.

"It's open!" Craig yelled, but Jerry chortled with demonic glee.

"No, it's locked! I locked it after you came in so no one would disturb us!"

With his hand still cuffed to Craig's, the policeman drew his pistol and aimed it at Jerry. Craig told him it wouldn't work. You can't kill someone who's already dead.

The flustered cop fired two shots anyway, hitting Jerry's torso point-blank but doing nothing. The ones in the hall heard the shots and saw everything on the monitor, and their attempts to breach the door intensified.

Craig said to Landry, "Run to the dumbwaiter and get away!" To the cop he said, "Unlock the cuffs. You'll die if you don't, and I can help you."

When he spoke, the moans and sighs in the room redoubled. Jerry screamed, "No one can help any of you, brother. You know that. Don't give them false hope."

"Unlock the cuffs!" Craig cried, and the cop, who was way out of his league on this one, complied. Landry grabbed a scalpel from the instrument tray and began hacking away at the tendrils as he sidled across the room toward the corner where the dumbwaiter stood open. He backed inside and slid the panel as far as he could, stomping and slashing vines until it closed. He pressed the down button, and as the car began to descend, the remaining vines disappeared.

It seemed an eternity as the dumbwaiter plodded along, and he spoke into the microphone.

"I'm coming down! Are you still in the office?"

The sheriff answered, "Still here. What the hell's going on up there? Were there gunshots?"

There was no time to answer. If Craig or Jerry opened the panel upstairs, the car would stop and trap Landry again. He shouted, "I'm getting off on the second floor. Go upstairs, now!"

He ran from the bedroom and flew up the stairs. Everyone in the hall had seen the vines evaporate after he entered the dumbwaiter, and he ran to Cate, who hugged him.

The two officers who'd been downstairs rushed over. "What's happening in there?" the sheriff shouted.

Detective Young yelled, "We must get that door open. How about shooting the lock?"

Landry said it wouldn't work because the doors were almost two inches thick.

THE EXPERIMENTS: THE BAYOU HAUNTING 5

"So how do you suggest we get in?"

"The window! We can go through the window." Three officers stayed outside the door while Landry took the others to the maintenance shed. They positioned the ladder and climbed it to the top of the second-floor porch. Then they hoisted it until it was next to the laboratory window. One cop scaled the ladder and waited while the others crept up behind him. The topmost man shattered the window, and they all scrambled up and into the room with Landry on their heels. The cops performed a drop and roll maneuver, coming up with pistols drawn but not knowing who or what to shoot at.

Things weren't going well at all. The New Orleans cop who had been cuffed to Craig now lay on the metal table in a cocoon. Only his face was visible as the vines spun like a maelstrom around his neck, and the pathetic man's eyes bulged out as he screamed for help.

"If you can't get me out, shoot me!" he pleaded. "Hurry. Please hurry! I'm suffocating!"

Landry ran to Craig and asked for the key, but he wasn't listening. He appeared to be in a fugue, but this time it was different. Before he had seemed distant and troubled each time, but now he focused on the bound man in the center of the room. Jerry emerged from the shadows, followed by the two dark specters that glided to the operating table.

Landry grabbed Craig and shook him hard. It worked for a moment — Landry saw a glint of recognition — but he turned away. Landry threw an arm around Craig's throat and squeezed, but in a burst of strength that surprised him, Craig pushed him backwards and broke free.

"What can we do?" someone shouted.

"Use your knives to cut the vines off him," Landry yelled. "Find anything that's sharp. Hurry before they suffocate him!" As he sprinted to the table to help, he saw Jerry turning knobs on the electroconvulsive shock machine. In seconds he heard the humming sound, and then he felt something cold against his face.

Craig stood behind him, holding the electrodes to Landry's temples. Landry lashed out, grabbed the two metal bars instead, and pushed them hard against Craig's head. He held them with all his might as Craig writhed and twitched, but in seconds he fell to the floor unconscious.

One of the darkened corpses raised its hand and pointed across the table at Landry. Jerry said, "Yes, Mother, I know you want him. We must keep our secrets."

As Jerry walked toward him, Landry shouted, "It's too late. Too many people know, and everything's on video. There are no more secrets now." He knelt, felt Craig's pants pocket and found the key. He ran to the door, unlocked it and threw it open. The five waiting in the hall rushed into the room, astonished to see in person what they'd been watching on the monitor.

"Help the guy on the table. Cut the vines off him!" Landry yelled, and two of the cops pulled heavy knives from their belts and began helping the others hack away the tendrils.

For a moment Landry forgot about Craig. When he looked, Craig wasn't on the floor. He yelled to the others, and several officers ran from the room to look for him.

Landry faced more immediate problems. Jerry was holding the orbitoclast — the pick-like instrument they used to perform lobotomies — and brandishing it like a spear toward the officers. One drew his firearm and took a step backwards as Jerry approached. When he raised the pick and prepared to strike, the cop fired two shots directly into his body.

The impact snapped Jerry's torso backwards, but it did nothing to stop him. He drove the sharp tool into the policeman's shoulder. He screamed in pain and swung with his other fist. The blow that connected with Jerry's cheekbone would have toppled a living man, but that wasn't what they faced here. As his fist hit Jerry's cheek, it didn't stop. It passed through the skin and into his face, slowing like it was sloshing through thick mucus. The astonished officer watched as the dead man's head erupted into a thousand disconnected parts and reformed as quickly as it had split.

It surprised the ones watching the video monitor to see Craig stride down the hallway. As they realized what he was carrying, they moved away. Cate called his name, but he was fixated on the laboratory door, throwing it open and shouting, "Leave him alone, Jerry! Let them all go. I'll give you what you want."

Jerry paused. He and the others turned to see Craig standing in the doorway, holding a two-gallon container of ethyl alcohol. Its lid was off, and some had slopped out on the floor.

"He's going to set the house on fire!" the sheriff shouted, but he was too far across the room to do anything. He drew his weapon, but he couldn't fire because Landry stood between him and Craig.

"Craig! Don't do it!" Landry screamed, taking a step toward him.

"No, Landry, stop! Don't come any closer. It has to be this way. I don't belong to your world any longer. Maybe I never have. I'm the product of my father and mother. I'm just like them."

As he raised the canister to shoulder level, the world seemed to move in slow motion. Landry stood transfixed, knowing he couldn't reach Craig in time to stop him from sloshing the flammable liquid around the room. He hoped it would be quick and prayed for Cate's safety. She was in the hall — perhaps she could get away before the fire spread.

Craig didn't do what they expected. Instead of dousing the room, he tipped the can toward himself, letting the clear liquid run down his body until the container was empty. He dropped it and raised his other hand.

Landry gasped when he saw the cigarette lighter. "No!" he shouted, diving toward him. But Craig was too quick. He flicked the lighter once, and his body exploded into a mass of swirling flames. Despite the horror he was enduring, he looked peaceful for the first time since Landry had met him.

CHAPTER THIRTY-NINE

Everything happened within a split second. Detective Young sprinted toward Craig at the same time Landry did, but when Craig set himself on fire, Young body-slammed Landry instead, deflecting his forward motion and knocking them away from the flames. As motionless and silent as a statue, Craig toppled to the floor. One of the cops dragged the heavy curtain over and threw it on him as two others leapt on top to smother the fire. The room and hallway were full of the shouts of police officers struggling to comprehend and deal with the situation. Cate ran to Landry, holding him in her arms and crying tears of joy that he survived.

They extinguished the flames, but there was no hope for Craig Morisset. Strips of roasted flesh hung from his face and arms. His hair was burned and his clothes charred. It had been a dreadful way to die, but what remained of his face still looked serene.

Landry could do nothing for Craig now. He went to the operating table where the officer lay and saw that the vines had disappeared. With everyone fixated on Craig's actions, the man had seen things they hadn't, and he appeared to be in a state of shock.

"Jerry...Jerry vanished," he mumbled, picking the orbitoclast off his chest and staring at it. "He was holding this over my face. He was about to stick it in my eye and he just vanished. The others too — those black ghosts or whatever. They're gone too."

Landry said, "They must have vanished the moment Craig died. He said that was what they wanted. I guess they sought retribution, and he gave it to them."

Phil and the director had stayed by the monitor, making sure the events were recorded instead of adding to the confusion in the laboratory. When it ended, Phil called everyone to the hall, saying there was something they should see.

His fingers flew across the keyboard as he brought up the live feed from the office downstairs. He hit rewind and found the place he wanted. "This shot is from thirteen minutes ago," he said as he pushed replay.

Craig walked into view, stood in front of the camera, and began to speak.

"Landry, I owe you an explanation, and this is the only way I can do it. You and the others are still upstairs. I tried to use the electrodes on you, but you turned them on me instead. I was only out for a few seconds, and I ran away because it was my only chance to get free and finish all this. Today is the end of the Morissets and the horrific acts we've committed for over a hundred years.

"My parents and my brother won't rest until I join them, and it has to happen now. I'm facing three counts of murder, and my defense is that the world was better off without them. I'll never set foot in my house again, and if I'm going to make things right, it must be now. I'm going to do it by self-immolation —" he held up the canister of alcohol "— and that's appropriate in these circumstances. I burned them to death, and now we'll be united when I die in the same manner. They will leave the house and go with me to the place where we're destined to spend eternity. I can only hope it's not as ghastly as the preachers say it is."

His face became a grimace as he continued. "The world knows Craig Morisset as a financial genius and wealthy philanthropist. Only my family knows the real person behind the facade. Someone else occupies my mind and my body, someone — or something — my father created when he twisted the instrument around inside my brain that day when I was ten years old. He removed the basic things a human needs — my conscience and sense of decency, my concern about doing the right things. Good and evil became merged in my newly tweaked mind, and I no longer took responsibility for anything I did. I told you I handed them the instruments during surgeries, but even that was a lie. I did a lot more than that. Much, much more.

"I have only a shred of morality left. It's taking every ounce of determination I have to convince myself what I'm about to do is the right thing. Selfishly I want to show the world I'm normal, but it's not true. I'm a twisted wretch with a broken brain. I'm sorry I ever came back to Jeanerette, I'm sorry I unleashed the horrors of my past, and I regret getting other people like you involved. Tell my story any way you wish. It's in your hands now. See you in the laboratory. Thank you, Landry, and goodbye."

Craig stepped out of view, and Landry listened to his footsteps as he walked into the hall to go upstairs, where he would kill himself a few minutes later.

Detective Young said to Landry, "Craig opened up to you about a lot of things. I've listened to the interview at Channel Nine, and now we've seen his final confession. You know more about him than anyone here. What do you make of all this?"

"I'm not sure how much I can help. He never opened up until towards the end, and I think this video is the first time he told the entire truth. I believe what he said about the conscience his parents took away from him. He felt no shame that he participated in horrific experiments on other human beings. He refers to a sliver of morality he had to cling to just to make this last confession. He knew what was coming soon — public disgrace and humiliation for him and his family by exposing them as sadistic murderers. By this evening's newscast, the name Morisset will be synonymous with Jack the Ripper. When our episode airs later, the public will see the rest of the story."

"You're saying he did this not because he was sorry, but to spare himself the humiliation?"

"That's right. The lobotomy turned off his morals. Today he chose to self-immolate and join his family instead of facing the consequences of his and their actions. He may say he did it to save everyone else, but to me he chose the coward's way out."

CHAPTER FORTY

While Cate returned to Galveston and resumed her own routine for a change, Landry traveled to Jeanerette several times over the next three weeks. He helped the investigators piece together what had happened at Amelia House and the laboratory in the woods. Once the authorities left, Landry's film crew took interior and exterior stills and video everywhere. They shot hours of footage with Landry standing in one room after another as he narrated the background material for the upcoming show. After editing there would be a two-hour special that looked to be a blockbuster for Channel Nine and Landry.

When the filming ended, Landry asked Cate to come over for a much-needed rendezvous. For weeks he'd had a packed schedule, and now it was time for them to be together, even if just for a long weekend.

He was waiting in the arrivals area at the New Orleans airport on a Friday night. After a long embrace and several welcoming kisses, they climbed into the black sedan Landry had hired for the evening. He had told her only that they were going upscale, so both of them dressed up a little.

They dropped her bag at his apartment, resisted the urge to shed both clothing and inhibitions, and headed out for their evening on the town. The driver took them to an intimate little place in the Faubourg Marigny district, where they sipped Sazeracs, listened to easy jazz, and caught up on things. Next it was off to dinner at Delmonico's, Emeril Lagasse's upscale establishment on St. Charles Avenue near Lee Circle. The hostess showed them to a quiet table, and the famous chef stopped by to welcome Landry and his date.

The time passed quickly, and at last they were alone at his place. They showered together, crawled into bed, and melted into each other's arms at last. They were asleep in minutes, but Landry woke a little after one and remembered that he'd muted his phone. He checked it. There was a call and voicemail from hours ago, and to avoid disturbing Cate, he crept into the living room to play it.

"Landry, this is Lieutenant Kanter. I'm in Key Largo, Florida, and we've found something I think you'll be interested in. I'll be working all weekend, so call when you can. I'll see you soon, because I guarantee you'll be heading this way once we speak."

Adrenalin flowing and all thoughts of sleep gone for now, Landry looked at his watch. 1:17 a.m. Too late to call.

He and the lieutenant had worked together on other cases, most recently the *Billy Whistler* incident in Vermilion Parish. They had a mutual respect and appreciation for their vastly different roles in the investigative process. Landry was scouting ideas for documentaries while Kanter was solving crimes, but they made a good team.

The state police had joined the Morisset investigation because kidnappings fell under their purview. Soon after Craig's death, he and Harry Kanter met at the mausoleum in Jeanerette to watch the local authorities unseal the crypts. Landry's crew recorded everyone's surprise, even though Craig had told them what to expect. There were empty places where the bodies of Craig's parents should have been. In the unmarked crypts were three, sometimes four bodies.

His mind racing, Landry crawled back into bed beside Cate and tried to fall asleep. Kanter's being in Key Largo made sense because that was where Craig kept his yacht. They must have found something while sorting through his possessions. He looked at the ceiling, wishing he hadn't missed the call.

He willed his mind to stop racing. At last he fell asleep, only to be awakened at six thirty by Harry's call.

Without apology for the early call on a Saturday, Kanter said, "You have to get down here fast. We've discovered something critical. So far, the local TV stations haven't figured out we're here, but once this gets out, this will be the lead on the evening news. You're going to want this story, and I need your help dealing with what we found. You've been in the middle of this case from the start, and you deserve first shot, so get down here ASAP."

Harry was a no-nonsense kind of cop. Honest, pragmatic and unemotional, he dealt with facts and didn't engage in idle speculation. For him to be in this mood, it must be something special for sure.

"Tell me about it."

"I don't have much time, because I'm meeting the others at the site in fifteen minutes. We discovered that Craig rented a storage unit in a false name. You're going to be surprised what we found inside. That's all you get. Come down here as soon as you can; I can't hold this for long. Tell me when and where to pick you up."

"It can't be where the bodies are buried," Landry quipped. "We already found those at the mausoleum."

"It's the next best thing. Trust me."

CHAPTER FORTY-ONE

When Cate came out of the bedroom, she found Landry working at his laptop.

"Morning," she said, not quite awake yet. "Is the coffee on?"

He said it was, and she asked how long he'd been up.

"Not long. Harry Kanter called and woke me up. I missed a message he left last night while we were at Delmonico's. He's on to something down in Florida where Craig lived, and he insisted I come immediately."

She poured a cup of coffee and sat down beside him. "And I'm sure you're going."

"He was gracious enough to give me advance notice of whatever it is. I'm thinking we both go. You were staying until Monday night anyway, so instead of spending the weekend here, come with me to the Florida Keys. We'll do a little investigating mixed in with some fun in the sun."

An hour later they were at the airport, and when they landed in Miami, one of Harry's men met them. On the way to Key Largo, Landry asked the cop what they'd found, but he said Landry had to talk to the lieutenant.

The officer brought them to a sixties-era motel on Overseas Highway called the Driftwood Inn. He parked in front of a downstairs room, and Harry came out to meet them. He shook Landry's hand and greeted Cate warmly. "I wasn't expecting you!" he told Cate, and she replied that she hoped it wasn't an intrusion.

"Not in the least. I apologize for interrupting your weekend, but I think you'll agree it's worthwhile. Come on in and I'll tell you what's going on."

Harry had rented two adjoining rooms, one of which was a bedroom. He'd turned the other into a workshop. Two cops were cataloging file folders, three-ring binders brimming with papers, and other things from transfer file boxes stacked on the beds. Dozens of boxes sat on the floor waiting to be examined. Each sealed box had an identifying label.

"We got a break," Harry said. "When we searched the boat, we found an envelope from a local storage company with a key inside. The manager recognized Craig from a photo we showed him, but he'd rented it under a different name. The only thing inside the unit were these boxes — thirty-seven of them. Looking at all this will take some time, as you can see. The ones we've opened so far contain records of the operations the Morissets performed. See those thick binders? Each of those covers one operation. They took incredibly detailed notes, enough to send them to the death chamber if any of them were around. The notes reveal where and how they snatched their victims, what they did with them before and after surgery — everything.

"Every binder contains the written confession of one of the Morissets. Looks like dozens of kidnapping and murder victims, all neatly cataloged and laid out for us. This should solve missing person cases going back a hundred years. I had the guys write down all the box labels. What we have here begins in 1909 and stops in 2003."

THE EXPERIMENTS: THE BAYOU HAUNTING 5

It made sense to Landry, given what Craig had told them. They started in 1909, and he killed his parents in 2003.

"It's quite a find," he agreed, "but it's all records. Now tell me what you need from me."

The lieutenant grinned like a Cheshire cat. "You can help with this box."

Landry looked at the label on the lid.

Craig Morisset. Personal and confidential.

"What's inside?"

"The pièce de résistance. According to the labels, every other box but this one has records of the operations they performed. When the boys showed me this label, I knew it might be important. I skimmed everything and I called you. You won't believe it."

Landry looked through the box. He sifted through file folders that held newspaper clippings and saw a lot of small books Harry said were Craig's personal diaries. At the bottom of the box lay a thick manila envelope. Someone had written "Craig Chastain Morisset. Last Will and Testament."

"There's a hell of a lot of stuff here. I have to go through this whole box, right?"

"Right. It won't take you long to understand why."

"Okay, Harry. You're way ahead of me. You've seen everything, so how about giving me a thirty-second teaser of what I'll find."

"Craig was nothing like what he made himself out to be. He wasn't the mistreated child who learned his family's horrifying secrets. He was an eager student who lured victims to his house so Frank and Maria could operate on them."

CHAPTER FORTY-TWO

"I feel sorry for him," Cate said. "Craig must have been a miserable human being from the day of his birth. He told us how hard he tried to make his parents like him. He tried to find out what they were up to so they'd care about him. Obviously, he did whatever it took; he even became one of them."

Landry agreed it was a tragic story. "Where should we begin?" he asked Harry.

"Start with the will. It'll let us know his thought process."

The manila envelope contained a cover letter from a law firm in Miami that had prepared the will almost a year ago. The two-page will began with the usual legal formalities, followed by Craig's declarations and the customary signature page.

Landry read Craig's declarations aloud.

If the world hasn't learned about what I am by the time I die, the following sentences should set things straight. I'm not a religious person, so the reader of my will can serve as priest, judge and jury. I do not intend to die a natural death. It wouldn't be right, considering what I have done and what I owe my parents. If I don't kill myself, then I trust my family will do it for me.

My father, Frank Morisset, performed a lobotomy on me when I was ten years old. While he was moving an instrument ever so slowly around in my brain, he managed to remove the essentials that make a person sane. He took away my morals, my conscience, my concern for doing the right thing and being a decent person. He must have been proud, because I could never have followed in his footsteps if I were a decent man.

Father missed a tiny part though, because I have a shred of principle, enough to realize what will be done upon my death.

I instruct my attorneys to use funds from my estate to burn down Amelia House. They are not to remove a single thing. Not one surgical instrument, or a medical book, or even a fork from the kitchen. Everything is to be incinerated and the debris hauled to a landfill and buried.

I hereby leave all my assets — the twenty acres on Bayou Teche and everything else I own — to St. Anne's College, Lafayette, Louisiana. It was the one place where I was accepted as a normal person, and where I spent the only four peaceful years of my entire life.

Cremate my body and flush the ashes down the toilet. I'll be in hell by then, spending eternity with all my relatives.

May what my great-grandfather started never be allowed to happen again.

They were silent for several minutes, reflecting on the heartbreaking confession of a tormented human being. He had done the right thing more than once. He had saved Landry's life. When they had read everything else in Craig's box, they would understand that the few good things he did were because of that shred of principle — that single bit of goodness his father missed.

THE EXPERIMENTS: THE BAYOU HAUNTING 5

The three-ring binders Harry Kanter showed Landry contained details about the victims, the operations and what happened to them, but the mementos in Craig's box allowed Landry and the others a glimpse into the harsh reality of Craig's involvement.

Craig wrote in his diary every day. Sometimes it was one line, other times two pages. The records began when he was twelve, two years after his lobotomy. Most were mundane thoughts, but Harry showed Landry the first significant entry Craig wrote.

A boy younger than Craig had shown up at the house. Craig caught him peeking in the windows, and the kid said he had heard there were ghosts inside. He lived across town and had walked there alone. Craig offered to give him a tour of Amelia House.

Harry handed Landry a newspaper article from June 1992 he'd found in the same box in a folder.

The headline said it all.

Searchers Comb Parish for Missing Jeanerette Youth

He handed over another. June 1993.

One Year Later, No Clue in Case of Missing Child

The day after Craig confessed at Channel Nine, every crypt in the Morisset mausoleum was opened. Eleven crypts had no nameplates, but as Craig had revealed, each held bodies. Even Jerry's space had three. The only empty spaces were those meant for his parents.

In those eleven crypts lay the bodies of thirty-six victims, including that of a nine-year-old boy from Jeanerette who disappeared in June 1992, and who became Craig's first contribution to the victim pool.

"These file folders are full of news articles," Harry said. "His grandfather started the tradition of accumulating the stories that came out when his victims disappeared. Craig's father and mother continued it, and Craig became the official family historian after his lobotomy. His diary records that on the days after his parents procured a victim,

Craig would ride his bike to Jeanerette and buy the newspaper that carried the missing person story. He carefully cut them out and put them in his folder, like any other kid might put a stamp into an album or put a prized baseball card into a shoebox."

Landry took Cate's hand. "How tormented his mind must have been. He told us so much, but there was so much he couldn't bear to reveal about his own involvement."

He looked at Harry. "Have you read all the entries?"

"Enough to know what I need to know."

"How many more were there?"

"He lured nine more to the house on his own. People trusted him because he was a boy. He wrote everything — every exhilarating high — in his diaries. He embraced his parents' work, Landry. His father taught him well, and he performed several operations on his own. He would even come back on college breaks and join them in the operating room."

Harry hadn't read the diaries, and now Landry wanted to delve into them. But as evidence they had to stay with Harry, so Landry and Cate spent the next several days in Key Largo.

CHAPTER FORTY-THREE

Ted sent Phil Vandegriff and a sound guy to Florida for a day to video Landry's work, the storage unit, the transfer boxes, Craig's will and the diaries.

During that week, between them Cate and Landry read every word of fourteen thick little books that laid bare the thoughts, feelings and twisted mind of Craig Chastain Morisset. Each time they came to a key entry, they flagged it, photographed the pages and read the passage aloud so they were both up to speed on everything Craig had done.

They also learned why thirty-seven boxes of records survived after he burned the laboratory to the ground. Craig was his parents' errand boy – the retriever of documents from the archives. At some point long ago, he started hiding things in his closet instead of returning them. When his parents were away, he'd move even more things to the house, apparently to have them close so he could study them later. The laboratory was crammed with materials and apparently his mother and father never realized he had secreted them. He was the one who had to bring things they wanted; if he had an item they requested in his closet, he'd merely go there and retrieve it.

Once they finished, Harry hauled everything from the storage facility back to Baton Rouge, where state police investigators would carefully match the victims to years of missing persons reports. Most were easy to find, and cold cases as far back as the nineteen twenties were solved, even though no one knew where their bodies were.

Albert had the mausoleum constructed in 1944 when his father, Marco, died, but he wouldn't store his victims' bodies there until the seventies. Nothing in the storage unit revealed where the Morissets disposed of the bodies before that. Landry told Harry they might have buried them near the laboratory building in the woods. That made sense, and the state cop sent earthmoving equipment out to Amelia House. It was a good hunch, and forty-one skeletal remains were removed from the ground, thirty-seven of which they would ultimately identify.

When added to the thirty-six they'd found in the mausoleum, there were eighty-seven victims in all. According to Craig's diaries, his father, Frank, killed twenty-six of them, ten of whom were lured to their deaths by Craig himself.

In the end they only had five left. Those were unfortunates who were drifters and whose families would never discover what happened to them.

The publicity surrounding the Morisset murders intensified the interest in Landry's latest *Bayou Hauntings* episode, "The Experiments." He'd toyed with calling it "Hell's Surgeons" — the term Craig used to describe his ancestors — but he couldn't bring himself to name a show after the men who committed those horrific crimes.

―――

One year later Landry and Cate stood on the banks of Bayou Teche along with several hundred others as a ceremony began. The president of St. Anne's University called the group to order, introduced the mayor, the governor and other dignitaries, and began the dedication that had brought these people together. Mothers and fathers, sisters and brothers of the Morisset victims stood in silence as eighty-two names were read aloud. Five more were nameless, but they were recognized too. Then a bell tolled eighty-seven times.

Craig had willed the property to his alma mater, but its board of regents knew the stigma attached to the Morisset family estate. They voted to create a park, its maintenance and upkeep funded in perpetuity by a few of the millions of dollars Craig had left to the school. There were benches for people to sit and watch boats on the river, and a playground for children.

Across the lawn lay a beautiful garden in the place where Amelia House stood before the wrecking crew took it down. Recently planted trees stood everywhere, and over a thousand multicolored flowers swayed gently in the breeze, silent sentinels to the things that had happened there.

They dedicated one last thing — a beautifully manicured cemetery on the banks of the Teche shaded by tall oak trees. A low wrought-iron fence surrounded eighty-seven graves, and there would be no more interments in this graveyard. At last each of the victims had a casket, and a tombstone, and a place to rest for eternity.

MAY WE OFFER YOU A FREE BOOK?

Bill Thompson's award-winning first novel, *The Bethlehem Scroll*, can be yours free.

Just go to
billthompsonbooks.com
and click
"Subscribe."

Once you're on the list, you'll receive advance notice of future book releases and other great offers.

Thank you!

Thanks for reading *The Experiments.*

I hope you enjoyed it and **I'd really appreciate a review on Amazon, Goodreads or both.**

Even a line or two makes a tremendous difference so thanks in advance for your help!

Please join me on:
Facebook
http://on.fb.me/187NRRP
Twitter
@BThompsonBooks

This is book 5 of The Bayou Hauntings Series. The first four (Callie, Forgotten Men, The Nursery and Billy Whistler) are also available as paperbacks or ebooks.

Printed in Great Britain
by Amazon